A FIERCE AND
SUBTLE POISON

A FIERCE AND SUBTLE POISON

SAMANTHA MABRY

Algonquin 2016

Published by
Algonquin Young Readers
an imprint of Algonquin Books of Chapel Hill
Post Office Box 2225
Chapel Hill, North Carolina 27515-2225

a division of
Workman Publishing
225 Varick Street
New York, New York 10014

LIBRARY OF CONGRESS CATALOGING-IN-PUBLICATION DATA
Names: Mabry, Samantha.
Title: A fierce and subtle poison / Samantha Mabry.
Description: First edition. | Chapel Hill, North Carolina :
Algonquin, 2016. | Summary: Spending the summer with his hotel-
developer father in Puerto Rico, seventeen-year-old Lucas turns
to a legendary cursed girl filled with poison when his girlfriend
mysteriously disappears.
Identifiers: LCCN 2015023792 | ISBN 9781616205218
Subjects: | CYAC: Supernatural—Fiction. | Poisons—Fiction. |
Love—Fiction. | Puerto Rico—Fiction.
Classification: LCC PZ7.1.M244 Fi 2016 | DDC [Fic]—dc23
LC record available at http://lccn.loc.gov/2015023792

10 9 8 7 6 5 4 3 2 1
First Edition

These pages are dedicated to the memory
of my granddaddy, Theron Wesley Mabry Sr., who fell
in love with a woman from Puerto Rico, and who would
have been tickled to have seen his name in a book.

A FIERCE AND
SUBTLE POISON

GREEN SKIN AND GRASS FOR HAIR

THE HOUSE AT the end of the street is full of bad air.

That's what the señoras always told us. They stuck their fingers in our faces and warned us not to get too close. They said it wasn't right that the shutters on the windows remained closed, even after rainstorms when the air was so thick it would rest on your skin and stick in the back of your throat. They said that the house had been cursed by the woman who once lived there. She hadn't always been bad, the señoras said, but her husband's constant neglect had left her hollow and wicked.

According to the old ladies, no one had ever trusted that man: he was white and a scientist. He was never in church. He walked the streets in the rain. He'd leave Old San Juan for weeks at a time and go out to the forests around Rincón, where he'd tear the legs off frogs, dissect live snakes to see their hearts beat out, or do whatever else it was that scientists did.

While he was gone, his wife was confined to the house.

She spent her days behind the three-foot-thick plaster walls tending to the plants in the courtyard and caring for the scientist's prized macaw. Everyone in town hated that bird. It never shut up. Every morning, it would jump onto one particular limb of a banyan tree and let out its ungodly screeches while its green and red feathers flickered like a pinwheel in the sun. Whenever someone walked by, the bird would slowly cock its head to an absurd angle, stare silently for a second or two, and then begin clucking blasphemous phrases, reciting lines from Borges stories, and singing songs nobody had ever heard before.

When I asked the señoras which lines from which Borges stories the gringo scientist taught his bird, they said they didn't know. It wasn't important. They curled their lips and asked why I would care about such a thing.

What *was* important, the señoras stressed with wags of their wrinkled fingers, was that the scientist was a very, very bad man. Somehow, somewhere, he'd lost all the beauty in his life, and that—that *loss*—was what caused him to rob his wife of all the beauty in hers. Everyone knew a Puerto Rican woman needed sun and wind and ocean water. But the scientist didn't care. He treated his wife like a creature under glass. He treated her like . . . the señoras always paused here for a moment . . . un especimén.

That's how life was for the woman who lived in the house at the end of Calle Sol until one summer, during which five hurricanes ravaged the island, battering the coastlines and tossing around telephone poles, a summer during which the scientist had again disappeared to the forests near Rincón to do whatever it was a scientist did. That was the summer things began to break apart.

The cracks in the exterior plaster walls came first, thick and meandering like the veins in an old woman's legs. Then the concrete of the sidewalk in front of the courtyard split, causing a mighty fissure a foot and a half wide. Aphids took over the garden. The macaw, perched up on its banyan tree, would spend hours plucking out his red and green feathers, letting them fall into the street one by one.

The woman's spirit was crumbling. And, as if out of sympathy, the house and the garden and the bird began to crumble along with her.

Around this same time, the people of Old San Juan all started having the same nightmare about a green skinned little girl who would stand in front of them and throw stones at their faces. After waking from fitful sleeps, they suffered further by having to listen to that *tonto* bird curse and croak out songs all day long. For months, they never had any peace. Then, one night in early December, the little green-skinned girl stopped haunting everyone's dreams. The following morning the scientist came home from Rincón to find his wife and his bird gone. The woman had taken nothing and left a curse. The bird's green and red feathers were scattered across the house. Only the plants in the courtyard remained.

That was the day the man closed all the shutters and

never opened them again, and that was the day all the birds in Old San Juan stopped flying over the house. They knew better than to get their wings tangled up in curses.

Over the years, my friends and I came up with our own stories about the house at the end of Calle Sol. Rico said the scientist's wife died after giving birth. She'd been in labor for five days, and after her husband held her green-skinned baby girl up to her face, she mumbled some prayers up to the saints. Then she kicked the bucket.

Ruben had a better version. He claimed the woman had been so upset by the fact that her husband was never around that she'd thrown herself off the highest of the stone walls of the massive old fort known as El Morro. It happened in the middle of the day, as dozens of people were out steering their kites through the wide blue sky. The last thing anyone saw was the woman's long black hair and the thin white fabric of her dress as she took a running leap. When the kite-flyers rushed over, expecting to see her broken body on the ledge many feet below, all they saw was a hibiscus bush with a single flower the color of fruit punch.

Carlos said he didn't know what happened to that *pinche* woman. All he knew was that every single one of the street cats knew better than to walk in front of that *pinche* house. Once, however, a tiny kitten, its eyes barely open, got separated from its mother and found itself alone on the sidewalk in front of the courtyard. The kitten mewed and mewed all night. The next morning someone found it curled up into a

4

ball, dead from chewing on a leaf that had fallen from the one of the tall bushes.

"Everybody knows," Carlos claimed, "that the plants in that courtyard are full of poison. If you touch them, they'll make your nightmares come true. Then you'll burn with fever. Then you'll die."

I thought the kitten story was bullshit. There are thousands of cats prowling around Old San Juan, and they could die for any number of reasons. The kitten could've been born sick and cast away by its mother. It could've had rabies. It could've eaten some of the chicken scraps Señor Guzmán mixes with glass and leaves out on the street in small piles to try to kill the ferals.

The summer I turned eleven, while we were sitting on a pier watching the cruise ships go by in the twilight, was when Rico claimed the scientist who'd lived in the house at the end of the street had a daughter and that she still lived there. He'd seen her. She was a little girl with green skin and grass for hair. He said he'd even talked to her. She'd told him she was a witch who could grant wishes.

We ran from the pier to my room at the hotel as fast as we could to scribble our wishes on the stationery the housekeepers kept stocked on my nightstand. It took Ruben the longest to figure out what his wish would be, but I knew mine right away. I wanted to lift the curse from the house, so that birds would fly over it again and the woman with the long dark hair would come home and throw open her shutters.

Once Ruben finally decided that his wish would be for his dead dog Pepé to come back to life, we folded our wishes in half, sprinted down to the end of Calle Sol, and tossed those wishes over the courtyard wall. The paper fluttered into the bad air and disappeared.

While my friends raced each other back to the pier, I stayed. I waited in front of the house to see if a bird would fly over and to listen for the sound of a woman crying. Nothing happened. And, as far as I know, none of our wishes ever came true.

One summer soon after, the stories stopped. Of course, the house at the end of Calle Sol was still there, still crumbling. The broken sidewalk had never been fixed. The blue paint was still chipped and faded, and the tops of plants still waved over the courtyard walls, trying to tempt me, but my friends and I had gotten too old to care about wishes, curses, and green-skinned little girls.

That's because there were other girls—*real* girls—whose bodies we could press against the walls of buildings in alleyways late at night. Up close, their skin smelled like warm, wet sand, and their mouths tasted like coconut water. They wore the thinnest cotton dresses with the tiniest straps we could slip off their shoulders, and their long dark hair was always curled from all the moisture in the air.

I was kissing one of those girls when the witch who grants wishes first threw stones at my face.

PART ONE

THE DISAPPEARED GIRLS

ONE

I MET MARISOL on a Sunday night, two days before her body washed up on Condado Beach. We were sitting across from one another in a field near El Morro drinking rum from a bottle I'd lifted from the hotel. She was one of Ruben's cousins, and he was there, too, along with Rico, Carlos, and some girls they all knew from school.

This is how things typically went: A girl would come over and run her fingertips across the back of my hand or the top of my knee. She'd look at me, her eyelids heavy, and say something about how her older brother or her uncle would kill me if they knew that she was hanging out with me. She'd mention my blond hair, my dad, and how she and the other locals didn't know whether or not he was saving their island or ruining it. She'd give me some version of some lesson she learned from her cousin in New York or Chicago or wherever about how white guys really know what it meant to treat a girl the way she deserves to be treated.

Eventually, I'd take her by the hand and lead her either into one of the narrow alleys between the Spanish-style buildings or down to the footpaths outside of El Morro near the ancient mangrove trees that reminded me of the gray ghosts of giants. In the attempt to convince her that I was cultured and interesting, I'd tell this girl about all the places I'd traveled and sights I'd seen. I'd tuck the stray hairs that fell in her face behind her ear. I'd be gentle, my touch featherlight. I'd look her in the eye and ask permission to kiss her.

She'd always say yes.

Marisol was different, though. She didn't mention anything about my blond hair or developer dad. She did come and sit by me, but after telling me her name, she said she remembered me from last summer, when she and Ruth—a giggling girl who was currently pawing at Rico—saw me at a party. She asked if I remembered her. I told her I did even though I didn't. Which was a shame. I should've. Marisol had a generous, loud laugh, a distinctive heart-shaped face, and straight, waist-length coffee-colored hair, the shade of which almost exactly matched her eyes.

She shifted onto her knees and nervously plucked at a blade of grass.

"I was hoping you'd come back," she said.

My head was already swirling from the rum, and I was only half listening. The way Marisol was sitting caused her butter-yellow dress to ride up high on her thighs. I wanted to reach out and touch the place where hem met skin.

"Let's take a walk," I suggested.

We snuck away and stumbled down a steep path that would lead us closer to the water. We faced a murky expanse of sea. Behind us was a section of the original walls of the city, built hundreds of years ago to protect San Juan from invaders. Forty feet up and on the other side of that wall was the dark and silent courtyard belonging to the house at the end of Calle Sol.

This spot was a favorite of mine, quiet and isolated. I could stand there for hours and wonder if I had the nerve to jump into that inky water and start swimming. When my arms got tired, I'd float. I sometimes couldn't imagine anything better than being alone in the ocean, carried along by the currents, with my arms out wide and the light from the moon and the sun bathing my face.

I never told any of the girls about my dreams of floating in the ocean. I also never mentioned how I always wondered if the wish on a scrap of paper I'd tossed into that nearby courtyard five summers ago was still up there, waiting to be granted.

"I grew up in Ponce."

Marisol's voice startled me, and I turned. She was leaning against the stone wall. Her fingers were lifted to her throat, where she was twirling a gold charm. It glinted twice in the moonlight. The rest of her was in shadow.

"My mom moved me and my little sister out here last May. I don't know if Ruben told you that or not." She shrugged. "I like it here, I guess."

Marisol dropped her charm as I approached her. I put my hand on her waist and felt the soft flesh under her dress give into my slight pressure. With my free hand, I brushed a strand of her hair away from her face and then ran my fingertips over one of the straps of her dress.

"So," I whispered, "you've been waiting for me?"

Marisol didn't even let the last word leave my lips before she grabbed the sides of my face and pulled my mouth to hers. Our rum-soaked lips collided and slid against each other's. Her hands were frantic and everywhere: in my hair, on my stomach, up the front of my T-shirt. I gasped as she raked her nails across the skin of my chest. When I threw my hands to the wall behind her to brace myself, she pressed her hips into mine and ran her teeth along the edge of my jaw.

I reeled back, needing a second to catch my breath.

Marisol's dark eyes were shimmering from the liquor and the moonlight, but I only caught a glimpse of them before she came crashing down on me again.

It was only seconds later, as I was grasping for the hem of Marisol's dress, when I felt something small and sharp run across my cheek. I thought it was one of Marisol's nails, until I realized her fingers were tugging at my belt loops. Something else pelted me on the shoulder, another on the top of my head.

I made the mistake of glancing up and was struck twice in quick succession, once in the center of my forehead and then again in the tender spot between my eyebrow and eye. Marisol shrieked and dodged away. I ducked and covered my head just as several tiny pellets showered down on me.

And then, everything was quiet. I knelt down, picked up a couple of the projectiles from around my feet, and rolled them around in my palm. They were stones, rough-edged and the size of small marbles.

I hurled them back up to their source and shouted. "Hey!" The stones came up short and rattled back down the wall. "Who's up there?"

I craned my head and was just able to make out the dark shapes of leaves swaying against a dark sky. Behind those leaves was something else, shadowed and stationary. There was a rustling noise, but that could've been from anything: the wind, a bird, a cat chasing a bird.

"That house is cursed," Marisol said, her voice slurred.

I lowered my gaze and gaped at her. She was still leaning against the stones. A strap of her dress had slipped down and was hanging loosely around her upper arm. Much of her dark hair had fallen like a curtain in front her face, and neither of us made an effort to sweep it back.

"That house is *cursed*," she said louder, as if I didn't hear her the first time. "That's what everyone says. Didn't you know that?" She swayed to the side and let out a short burst of laughter.

Again, I peered up to the top of the wall. It was the same

as before, as it always had been, dark objects against a dark sky, leaves and branches bending in the breeze. I shivered as an unexpected rash of goose bumps rippled up my arms.

"Come on." I extended my hand to Marisol. "Let's go."

"You're bleeding," Marisol replied, pointing at my forehead. "Like, a lot."

I swiped at my eyebrow, and sure enough, my trembling fingers came away slick. I wiped them off on my jeans and snatched Marisol's hand.

"It's fine," I said. "Cuts like these always look worse than they actually are." There was a wobble in my voice; I hoped she didn't notice.

I could feel the blood from the cut trailing down the middle of my face and dripping from the tip of my nose, and going up the steep steps while drunk was giving me the spins. Once Marisol and I got back to the field, I could just make out Rico in the near distance, acting the carefree clown as usual, trying to dance to nonexistent music and continuously toppling over. Everyone was laughing, except for Carlos, who was sprawled out on the grass, snoring with his mouth wide open.

When we got close enough for Ruben to see my face, he sneered and asked what I'd done to make Marisol sock me. I rolled my eyes and Marisol erupted into a fit of giggles. Neither of us mentioned the rain of stones.

I drank more rum as the night went on. I acted as if Rico's antics were the most hilarious thing I'd ever seen and that

Marisol's attention was all I'd ever need. I acted this way because I didn't want to let on how I couldn't stop thinking about that one dark shape I'd seen on top of that courtyard wall, the one I didn't mention to Marisol, the one that didn't sway like the leaves but that seemed focused solely on me and was poised in a motionless crouch, ready for a reason to jump.

TWO

"ROUGH NIGHT?"

My dad was talking at me from behind the pages of the morning's *El Nuevo Día*. It wasn't even seven o'clock, but he was already up and dressed for what my mom used to refer to as the "island life." His outfit consisted of a white linen suit, a light blue dress shirt, and tan boat shoes. His graying hair was slicked back with pomade. His wide-brimmed hat was balanced on his knee. He thought he looked debonair. I thought the only thing missing from the picture was a cigar and a mountain of cocaine on the table in front of him. Behind his back, my friends would snicker and refer to him as el patrón or, when they were feeling particularly brutal, el conquistador.

Aside from the tourists who came in on cruise ships, no man in Puerto Rico ever dressed for the "island life" like my dad did. Some of the older men wore guayaberas, those cotton, button-down shirts with the pocket patches running down the front, and most had wide-brimmed hats, though theirs probably didn't cost close to a thousand dollars. I just wore jeans or cargo shorts, white V-neck T-shirts, and flip-flops or Converse. My friends wore more or less the same. Unlike my dad, I didn't dress to impress; I dressed to avoid being drenched in sweat immediately upon stepping out the hotel doors.

Not that I'd be stepping out the hotel doors anytime soon. I wouldn't have even dragged my ass out of bed this bright morning had it not been for mine and my dad's "standing breakfast."

The rum from the night before had become a painful fog in my head. I remembered that Jorge, the night doorman, had dragged me by my armpits up to my second-floor room, where I'd passed out and dreamed of a little girl with green skin standing in front of me, throwing stones at my face. The stones kept hitting louder and louder. Eventually I realized there were no stones. It was morning, and someone from the front desk was pounding on the door because I hadn't answered my wake-up call. I finally peeled my eyes open enough to see that I was face down on the floor in front of my bed, fully clothed, having managed to remove only one of my shoes before passing out. The phone was ringing in such a loud, high pitch I was tempted to yank it out of the wall and hurl it across the room. But before I could do that, I'd run to the bathroom and puked.

So yeah, it had been a rough night.

The waiter came by and sat a plate of watery scrambled eggs in front of me, and I nearly puked again right there. I had to look up, away from my food, to the tops of the palm trees rustling over the open-air courtyard. Their motion against the blue sky was soothing.

"Juan," I heard my dad say to the waiter, "how long ago did you brew this coffee?"

"Just before you came in, señor," Juan replied. "As we usually do."

"It doesn't taste very fresh. Please brew another pot."

The waiter shuffled away mumbling a half-hearted apology. My dad abandoned the first question he asked me—because the answer was obvious—and shot me another.

"Have you thought any more about where you want to do your college visits?"

I hadn't. He knew I hadn't. We both had a common understanding that so long as I didn't prove myself totally incompetent, upon graduation from wherever I went, where I would get whatever GPA, I'd be handed a position at my dad's firm in Houston, quickly rise through the ranks, and be able to spend my summers out here in the Antilles. I wanted a shack on some remote beach where I could spend my days alone. Very infrequently, I would leave my shack, drive around the island with my assistant, and say things like, "Build a resort there. Make sure the decor is chic and modern. Make sure it's eco-conscious. People love that kind of thing these days."

Ignoring my dad, I looked back to my plate, picked up a slice of cantaloupe, nibbled the flesh, and then tossed it back down.

"Lucas."

My dad had placed his folded paper across his empty plate. This meant it was time for him to impart some of his precious wisdom upon me.

"What happened to your face?"

My face. Right. I reached up, felt around gingerly with the pads of my fingers, and winced at a sore spot just above my eye. I remembered more of last night: the stones, the shape perched at the top of the wall. I took a sip of water; it had a metallic tang.

"I fell near El Morro," I replied, poorly covering up a gag.

My dad sighed. "I'm all for you having a good time with your friends, Lucas, but let's try to bring it down a notch." A fly buzzed around his head, probably attracted by the sweet smell of his pomade. "Jorge told me about you coming home at three-thirty in the morning, tripping over your own feet and ranting about some girl who cursed you." He leaned closer and lowered his voice. "I don't know what it is you do all night long, aside from hang out with local kids and get drunk on *my* rum, but I'm warning you about getting into personal relationships with island girls, if you understand what I'm saying."

Oh, I understood what he was saying. And if I'd had a clearer head, what I said next might never have left my lips.

"Mom was an 'island girl.' You got into a 'personal rela-tionship' with her."

My dad responded in slow motion. First, he set his porce-lain coffee cup back on its saucer. Then he placed the saucer on the glass top of the table. Leaning back in his seat, he fin-gered the brim of his hat as he decided what to say. He could tell me to watch my smart mouth. He could laugh and say *touché.* He could brush it off, blaming my hangover. Or he could change the subject to one less off limits.

"I'm looking out for you." He grimaced as he pinched a minuscule piece of lint from his hat. "I only wish that some-one would've cared enough to give me that same bit of advice before it was too late."

While my dad took his hat off his knee and rose to stand-ing, I tried to not interpret his remark as him regretting my very existence. He pulled his mirrored Ray-Ban aviators from his jacket pocket and slid them on before checking his reflection in the glass of the table and giving himself a satis-fied smirk.

El patrón.

"I'm going to Rincón tomorrow," he said. "I'll be gone for the night and most of the next day. I'll leave the address with the front desk before I go if you decide you want to take a car and meet me. I know you've always liked it out there, though I still can't understand why."

Rincón was less than a hundred miles from San Juan, but seemingly another world. To me, it was beautiful just as it was, all trees and big, big waves. My dad thought differently, though. To him, Rincón was some indigent fishing village where mainland hippies went to surf and get high. He couldn't wait to build a hotel out there and help give the town a "touch of class," as he liked to say. It didn't hurt that he'd make a fortune in the process.

My dad and I, like the scientist at the end of Calle Sol, are gringos. And just like no one ever trusted the scientist, no one trusted us. Every summer since I was ten, the two of us would come to San Juan from Houston and stay at this luxury hotel that his company had converted from an old convent. Every morning of every summer, after reading his newspaper, drinking his coffee, and eating his pan dulce and melon, my dad would get into the backseat of a big black car and be gone until sundown—out looking for other old buildings to convert to hotels or the perfect place on the beach on which to build from scratch. I'd spend my time roaming around the hotel by myself and playing out in the streets with the three Old San Juan kids who would give me the time of day. It was from those kids' abuelas, mamás, and tías that I learned all of my stories about the island. They told me their stories, but they never trusted me. They smiled but never really meant it. Their whispers and suspicious stares always broke my heart.

My dad was making his way to the other side of the courtyard just as Juan brought a fresh urn of coffee. Leave it to Michael Knight to complain, make a demand, and forget he did either.

"Sorry about that," I muttered with a pained smile. "But I'll take some, please. And hey, Juan?" He cocked his eyebrow but didn't look at me as he continued pouring the coffee. "Do you know if someone recently moved into the old house at the very end of Calle Sol?"

Juan did a strange thing: he laughed. It started as a chuckle but quickly shifted into a full-on, open-mouthed, head-tipped-to-the-sky guffaw. Then he turned and walked away, shaking his head and wiping the tears from the corners of his eyes.

I downed my cup of black coffee as quickly as I could and left the table without touching any more of my breakfast. Up in my room, I managed to get both of my shoes off before collapsing on top of the covers. If I dreamed of anything, I couldn't remember what it was.

That night, Marisol's head was in my lap while my fingers explored the cool strands of her long hair. We were in Ruben's bedroom with the group from the night before, half watching some American reality dating show because it was the only thing coming in on the antenna.

Ruben was downing can after lukewarm can of Medalla and shouting insults at the television. On a tattered loveseat on the other side of the room, Rico was feeling up Marisol's friend Ruth.

"I'm sorry about what happened last night," Marisol said

before taking a sip from a straw that was plunged deep into a glass Coke bottle. "I had *way* too much to drink. I hope I didn't say anything too embarrassing. If I did, just pretend it didn't happen."

I smiled. She really was pretty; I hadn't really noticed the night before. Her eyes weren't purely coffee-brown after all. They were flecked with green and hazel, which gave them a wild quality.

A gold charm in the shape of the letter *M* rested between her collarbones, where her skin was slick with sweat. It was hot in Ruben's house even though the sun had set and even with the creaky ceiling fan whipping above our heads at full speed.

"Mari!" Ruben cried out, pointing at the television. "You can be honest with me since we're family and all. Tell me. What is it with this guy? He looks like he and Lucas could be brothers. What is it about skinny blond white guys that make all the girls line up, huh?"

"Don't answer that, Marisol," I said.

"I don't see a line of girls here for Lucas," Marisol replied before taking another sip of Coke.

Ruben grunted and took a pull from his beer can. "You haven't been around for long enough then. They line up."

"We should take a walk," I suggested to Marisol. "You want to take a walk?"

She narrowed her eyes at me and then craned her head

to shoot a worried glance at the hot tangle of limbs that was Ruth and Rico.

"They'll be fine," I said. "We won't be gone long."

The old town was mostly deserted. Once outside of Ruben's house, I steered Marisol into a nearby alley off San José Street, gripped a fistful of the fabric of her floral-print sundress, and pulled her close. Again, and without the rum swimming in our heads, we kissed. When my lips left her mouth and traveled down her throat to land between her collarbones, where the little gold *M* settled against her skin, I felt her tremble. She whispered in my ear how much she was hoping to see me again and then plunged her hands into my hair.

It was later, as we walked together through the empty streets, that Marisol told me about her dream of moving to America once she finished high school. She was even considering dropping out. Her goal was either to open a café or play French horn for a symphony somewhere. She'd never played French horn before, she said, but she was convinced she could learn. It had been her favorite instrument ever since she found out it was the Wolf in *Peter and the Wolf.*

She asked me what Texas was like and if I'd been to any of the big cities like Los Angeles and New York. I told her I had, but when I said I thought they were too big, too noisy, and too full of people, she seemed disappointed.

"Ruben was right, you know," she said, hooking her pinky

finger with mine. "I haven't been around San Juan very long. My mom and I and my sister Celia moved up from Ponce just over a year ago." She'd said that last night, almost word-for-word, but I didn't remind her of it. "I like it here better. There's more to do. The rest of my family's here, and my mom has a better job."

We turned onto Calle Sol. In the middle of a large circle of light cast by a street lamp, an orange cat was grooming himself on the sidewalk.

Marisol saw it and smiled a close-mouthed smile.

"Celia wants to take home every cat she sees. Even though they all hiss when she runs up to them, she calls them her babies. Are you taking me back to the same place you took me last night? By the water?" She paused, but not long enough for me to get a word in. "It's not that it matters. I just can't be out as late as I was last night. My mom'll kill me. She's been worried ever since that American girl went missing over in Condado . . . Sara Something."

"Fikes," I replied.

According to the news, sixteen-year-old Sara Fikes went out a couple of nights ago to take pictures of the sunset and never made it back to the beachfront hotel room where she was staying with her parents. When the police began searching for her the next morning, they found her flip-flops and her Nikon placed neatly on the sand half a mile down the coast, as if she'd set them there before going out for a quick swim.

"Where's *your* mom?" Marisol asked. "All I ever hear

anyone talk about is your dad. Did you know they call him el patrón?"

Yes, I knew that.

"Does el patrón have una patrona?" she urged.

"My mom's not around." I paused. "I haven't seen her in years."

"En serio?" Marisol clasped my hand and forced me to stop. "I'm sorry, Lucas. If I had known that, I wouldn't have asked. No one told me."

"Don't worry about it." I forced the side of my mouth up into a half-smile. "It is what it is, I guess. She's been gone for so long, I barely remember her."

That wasn't quite true, but I wished it were. My mood tended to sour when I talked about my mom, which isn't what I wanted to happen while I was with Marisol. She was different than I was: full of optimism and hope and brightness.

We walked on. For a while it was so quiet, I could hear Mari's sundress swish around her legs. I had the sense she thought that by bringing up my mom she'd tread unknowingly into a minefield and was searching for a way to retrace her steps. Eventually, she stopped. Her gaze had landed on something down the dark street, and I watched as a small smile spread across her face.

"What?" I asked.

Marisol pointed to the scientist's house. I'd brought us straight to it without even realizing it.

"The other day my grandma told me that house is cursed," she said, again repeating herself from last night. "It was some stupid story that another old lady at the market told her—about how anyone who goes into the house never comes out and that maybe the man who lives there eats them or something."

I laughed. "*Eats* them?"

"Yes, eats them." Marisol nodded soberly. "He puts them in a big pot with carrots, onions, and potatoes, and lets them simmer overnight. Have you not heard that?"

"I haven't heard *that*," I said. "But I heard that the house was cursed, yeah."

I told Mari the señoras' story about the scientist who kept his wife trapped with his bird and his plants, and also about how when we were kids my friends and I would make up our own stories.

"Rico said that a witch lived there and if you wrote a wish on a piece of paper and threw it to her, she would grant it."

"Did you throw a wish?" Marisol asked. I tried to hide the truth but the strained expression on my face apparently gave me away. "You did!" she exclaimed, clapping her hands. "I know you did. What did you wish for?"

I shook my head. "I can't tell you. Only the witch knows."

Marisol let out a cry of mock-outrage just as the orange tom behind us expelled a guttural screech. I turned just in time to see it zip down a nearby alley.

Marisol released her hand from mine and ran over to the

wall of the scientist's courtyard. She picked at a flake of loose plaster with her fingernail and peered up at the tips of the leaves.

"This is where the stones came down from last night, right? I remember that! *Someone* has to be there or else all these plants would die. Come on, Lucas." She reached down to slip off her sandals. "Give me a boost. We'll solve the mystery, and then we'll get to tell all the old ladies what the *true* true story is. If I don't come back, just tell them I was eaten. They'll understand."

I was impressed. As long as I'd been coming to the island neither me nor any of my friends had ever thought of actually going *into* the scientist's house. It had always been a place people judged from far away and made up stories about, not a place they would ever willingly enter.

"That wall is three feet taller than you," I said, offering up the most rational response—one that didn't involve poison or witches or curses. "Even if I gave you a boost, there's no way you'd ever get back over."

"There might be a ladder or something on the other side." She stood on the balls of her feet and stretched her arms up to the sky. As much as she was willing herself to be a giant, it wasn't happening. "A little help, por favor."

"You *just* said something about not wanting your mom to worry about you and now you want to jump into a house that's cursed." Marisol ignored me and started taking little two-footed leaps into the air. She still came up very short.

"You look ridiculous, by the way. Whatever you're trying to do isn't working."

Marisol let out a burst of laughter and finally stepped away from the wall. As she put her sandals back on, one of the straps of her dress fell off her shoulder. I stepped closer and lifted it back in place.

For a moment, the tips of my fingers lingered against her warm skin. They traced the curve of her shoulder up to her throat. She leaned in, brushing her lips across my ear.

"Paper," she whispered.

I jerked back. She was grinning. It was a devilish expression, made even more devilish by the mixed light from the moon and the orange-tinted street lamps.

"Do you? Have any? *Pay*-per?" she asked. "I want to make a wish. You can't object to that. It's something you've done yourself."

"When I was a kid, yeah."

She shook her head. "Doesn't matter. Do you have paper or not?"

I dug into my pockets and pulled out a quarter, a couple of crumpled receipts, and the folded piece of hotel stationery on which my dad had scribbled the name and address of the place he'd be staying in Rincón. He'd written the information just under the embossed logo he was so proud of, a blood-red palm tree, and the name, Hotel St. Lucia.

Marisol snatched the piece of stationery from my hand and began to dig through her small, tooled leather purse. She pulled out a pen with a squeal of triumph, placed my dad's note on her knee, and scribbled her wish on the back. She then wadded the paper up into a ball and pitched it over the wall.

"Do you want to know what I wished for?" she asked, twirling toward me.

"Yes, but don't tell me."

"That's okay." Marisol gripped my hand and started to lead me back down Calle Sol in the direction of Ruben's house. "Only the witch knows now."

THREE

AFTER HAVING A tense, chat-free breakfast with my dad bright and early the next morning, I went down to a jewelry shop in the touristy section of San Juan and bought Mari a charm for her necklace: a dime-sized head of a wolf, cast in pewter, in honor of her dream of playing French horn. The plan was to give it to her when I returned from Rincón in a couple of days.

Back in my room, I was lying on my bed flipping mindlessly through the channels when I landed on the news and the familiar headshot of Sara Fikes. The press apparently had only one picture of her, and they showed it something like seven times every thirty minutes, along with the phone number they'd set up for tips. In the photo, Sara was wearing a bright red jersey and holding a volleyball in the crook of her arm. Her long, board-straight dark hair was neatly swept over one shoulder. Her smile was toothy, forced-looking, like she'd been holding it too long and her jaw was getting sore.

"Police have expanded their search to include Santurce and some of the other outlying districts," the television buzzed. "Meanwhile, Fikes's parents vow to not return to Florida until their daughter has returned safely."

Puerto Rican girls went missing all the time, and their faces were rarely on the news. The señoras referred to them as desaparecidas, the disappeared girls, and their stories always made the señoras cry when they told them. The desaparecidas were just ordinary girls who vanished from their beds or when they were walking home at night. The police did little to find them, and mostly assumed them to be runaways. Despite their families' desperate pleas to God and the hundreds of votive candles lit in their honor, none of the girls were ever seen again—unless it was by Señora Gaona, who everyone said had gone loca after her third stroke. She sold fruit down at the Plaza de Mercado, and she swore that one night, years ago when she was going home from her daughter's house near Condado Beach, she saw a teenage girl standing on the sidewalk, looking like she'd walked straight out of the ocean. Her hair was wet. Her feet and ankles were speckled with dried sand. Señora Gaona claimed she called out to the girl, asked her where she lived, but the girl didn't answer. She told the girl to stay right there, that she was going for help, but by the time she'd come back with her son-in-law, the girl was gone.

I've heard Señora Gaona tell the story about the night she found the disappeared girl at least a dozen times. Each time, she'd look up to the sky, her eyes sparkling with tears, and recall how the air that night smelled of cinnamon and salt water.

My dad was also convinced that the desaparecidas were runaways, but no matter what he or the police said, I believed the señoras. I never thought their stories were just stories. And while Señora Goaona seemed a little batty, she never struck me as a full-blown liar.

Sara Fikes's disappearance, however, was a different story. Since she was from the mainland, the cavalry got called in, and the police were doing "everything in their power" to reunite her with her parents.

I couldn't help but think, though, that the thing with the camera was strange. She'd really just set it down and walked barefoot into the water? And the last photo she'd taken—what was it of?

I must've dozed off, because the next thing I remember is waking up with the remote in my hand and the lights, the television, and all my clothes still on. My stomach hissed. It was 2:00 p.m., time for lunch.

I swung my legs off the bed, and something on the ground caught my eye. One of the staff had slipped a piece of hotel stationery under my door while I was asleep. I crouched down to pick it up and saw three distinct sets of handwriting.

The first belonged to my dad: *Hotel de las Palomas, 24 Via San Angelica, Rincón.* When I turned the paper over,

I noticed a scrawl of blue pen that must have belonged to Marisol: *I wish.* But whatever it was she'd wished for was illegible, crossed out by a series of heavy black lines. The third set of writing was in an unfamiliar, perfect cursive:

Sorry, Lucas, it read. *This is one I just can't grant.*

FOUR

I STUDIED THE web of creases spread across the piece of paper. Whoever had crossed out Mari's wish had pressed down into the paper hard enough to create indentations. They hadn't just wanted to erase her wish; they'd wanted to obliterate it.

On television, the newscasters were talking about the weather.

"Better hunker down," they were saying. "Storms are coming."

I picked up the phone on my nightstand and with shaky fingers dialed Marisol's number. Her grandmother answered. "Mari no está!" she yelled into the receiver. "She's probably with Ruth. My Mari is too good to be hanging out with that girl. She never asks about my health. She has bad manners."

As I hung up, someone knocked on my door.

"Lucas! You up?"

It was Carlos, his voice muffled through wood.

I shoved the note into my back pocket and went over to open the door. In one fluid motion, Carlos plowed right past me, undid the buttons of his porter's uniform, kicked off his shiny leather shoes, and collapsed onto my unmade bed. Then he grabbed the remote from the nightstand and started to flip through the channels.

"Sorry if I woke you," he said.

I loved Carlos like a brother, but his timing couldn't have been worse. All I wanted to do was find Marisol and figure out who crossed out her wish. I couldn't shake the image from my head of a little girl with green skin and grass for hair, sitting in the courtyard of the house at the end of Calle Sol, sucking on leaves, waiting on wishes to land in her lap.

"No you're not," I replied, closing the door.

"You're right, I'm not." He spread out his limbs, creating an *X* across the mattress. "Ay, this bed!" Carlos's eyes closed in rapture. "Lucas, you have no idea how good you've got it."

Earlier in the summer, Carlos had asked me if I could get him a job at the hotel. He said he'd do anything: wash dishes, clean toilets, get down on both knees and kiss the tourists' butts. All he wanted was to save enough money to get a one-way ticket off the island so he wouldn't end up like his dad, working as a waiter out on the cruise ships for the rest of his life. A part of me hated seeing one of my best friends scurrying around the hotel in his bright white porter's uniform and squeaky black shoes, saying *yes, sir* and *no, sir*, carrying suitcases up and down staircases and catering to every ridiculous request of every ridiculous guest, but he didn't seem to mind it. He was the only one of our group who had a regular job, and every once in a while he'd celebrate his gainful employment by buying us all salt cod fritters and soda from the street vendors down by the pier.

"You on a break or what?"

My voice had an edge to it, but Carlos either didn't notice or didn't care. He took one of my pillows and shoved it under his head.

"No. I'm done. I worked the early shift. I'm telling you, this place is loco. You would not believe the shit that goes on down here."

"You didn't run into anyone that was looking for me, did you?"

"Nah." Carlos turned onto his side so that he was facing me. He pushed his pomaded hair back into place and grinned like a little kid with a big secret. "But get this. This woman calls the desk this morning asking for towels, right? So I go down to housekeeping, get four of the whitest, fluffiest towels for this woman's white, fluffy ass, and I go knock on the door. She answers—I swear to you—naked." He paused, I assumed to allow me time to draw up a mental image. "No clothes."

Carlos rolled onto his back and put his hand over his brow

as if the memory was in the process of undoing him. "Madre de Dios!" he cried out to the ceiling, "I will remember the shape of that woman's beautiful breasts until the day I die."

I couldn't help but a crack a smile. "So what, she just took the towels and thanked you like it was no big deal? Did she at least give you a tip?"

"My friend, what she gave me . . . " Carlos closed his eyes and tapped his temple twice. "What she gave me is something you can't measure in dollars and cents. But, hey." He sat up and checked the clock on the nightstand. He seemed far too full of energy to have just come off a ten-hour shift. "It's early enough that we can make it to the market before Señora Mendoza runs out of pan dulce and then go to the beach before the sun goes down. What do you say?"

As he leaned over to lace back up his butt-kissing shoes, I faltered.

"Are you coming or what?" Carlos asked. He jumped to standing and fiercely rubbed the palms of his hands together like a person does if he's either standing over a fire or hatching some magnificent plan. "After what happened this morning, I've got a good feeling about the rest of the day. Quesitos and coffee on me."

With so much raw hope shining from his eyes, it was impossible for me to refuse.

We shared a cab the five miles from Old San Juan to the Mercado. Once there, I followed close behind Carlos as he shouldered his way through the large crowd. Our destination was a tiny blue pushcart with a frayed giant yellow beach umbrella that sat among dozens of other fruit and vegetable stands. From the look of sheer determination on his face, you'd think Carlos was after a long-lost love rather than an eighty year-old woman selling pastries. He was convinced that Señora Mendoza, who got up at four o'clock every morning to crank up her gas oven, whip together her cheese filling, roll out layer after layer of pastry dough, and then push her cart down the street to the market, was proof that God existed and had designed our stomachs to be filled with sweets.

We were waiting in another line for coffee, our hands and mouths dusted with powdered sugar from the quesitos, when I turned at the sound of someone calling my name. It was Ruben. He was squeezing through the crowd in our direction, holding several shopping bags with one hand. In his other hand he was grasping the palm of a little girl—obviously Celia, given her resemblance to Marisol. Her dark brown hair was pulled up into two symmetrical pigtails, and she was wearing a sepia-toned sundress. As the two approached, I could see the little girl's cinnamon eyes burning with impatience. She was a shifty one, scoping out the corners of the market as if trying to find an exit. Ruben was sweating through his white T-shirt and seemed thoroughly miserable.

"Didn't expect to see you here," Carlos said before taking

the first bite of his second quesito and releasing a puff of white powder around his cheeks.

"Where'd you get that?" the little girl asked Carlos. "Ruben, can I . . . ?"

Ruben gripped the girl's hand until she squealed.

"I'm stuck with Celia *all day*," Ruben griped. "Mamá y Tía went down to Ponce. Marisol was supposed to watch her, but no one knows where she went off to." He lifted his forearm to wipe back the short chunks of sweaty hair that were stuck to his forehead. "I was thinking she might have been with you, Luke."

"No," I replied. "I haven't seen her since last night."

"We were going to the beach," Carlos said. "Why don't you two come?"

Ruben shook his head. "Celia can't swim. She's afraid of the water."

"Ruben, shut up!" Celia hissed.

"Es la verdad!" Ruben exclaimed. He knelt down in front of his little cousin and whispered to her in Spanish too rapid for me to understand.

"We can take turns," I offered. "I don't mind watching her on the beach while you guys swim. Celia and I can hunt for shells or something. We'll dig up a present for her sister."

Ruben swiveled his head and sized me up for a second.

"Won't that be fun, Celia?" he asked, his enthusiasm obviously faked.

Celia didn't respond. She'd gotten distracted by a woman

and her black-and-white cattle dog performing tricks for change in the middle of the square.

"So," Carlos said, "what are we waiting for?"

Just like in the hotel, I hesitated. The combination of the note stuffed in my pocket and not being able to get ahold of Marisol was making me more and more anxious. But I also didn't want to come across as some possessive creep demanding to know every single move of a girl I'd just met. Ruben didn't seem worried, just pissed that he'd been saddled with Celia. *Mari's fine*, I told myself. *She's with Ruth.*

"Let's go," I said. "Before it gets too late."

We made our way through the more run-down neighborhood of Santurce and passed underneath a highway before hitting Avenida Ashford, the busy, upscale street where all the luxury beachfront high-rise hotels sat. During that time, Carlos told Ruben the story about the lady with the towels, going so far as to silently act the parts that he felt would be inappropriate for a seven year-old to hear. At one point Ruben was laughing so hard he had to stop and set down his bags in order to collect himself.

Once the beach was in sight, I hoisted Celia up onto my shoulders, where she gripped my chin with her chubby fingers. I twisted my head up to see her eagle eyes focused on the shore.

"There's something wrong!" Celia shouted. She released one of her hands and pointed in the direction of the beach. "There are ambulances near the water. I can see their lights."

Carlos, Ruben, and I shared a glance. All three of us were thinking the same thing. Someone had gone out for a late-night or early-morning swim and had fallen victim to the currents. That happened sometimes, maybe once every couple of years, but usually when the weather was much worse, causing the sea to tumble like a furious machine.

Today the sky was clear and bright, almost a postcard-perfect shade of azure.

We skirted around the side of one of the hotels and got as close to the shore as we could. Access to the beach, however, was blocked by police tape. Small crowds of locals had formed; word of mouth had worked in its typical swift and efficient way. Beyond the crowd and closer to the water, the lights of squad cars and the ambulances silently flashed. Several television reporters stood at the ready in front of their cameramen with microphones in hand. From the balconies of their sea-facing rooms, tourists pressed against the railing. Somewhere not too far away, a dog was barking.

As we merged with the rest of the onlookers, I heard some of them murmuring, praying, speculating. I lowered Celia from my shoulders, and her feet sank into the sand.

Ruben stood up on his toe-tips and raised his chin, trying to peer over the shoulders and between the heads of the people who had gotten there before us. None of us could see much.

"We can try La Andalusia," Carlos suggested, pointing

to the barely visible white shell of a high-rise with torn and faded red awnings several hundred meters down the beach. "We can probably get a better view from there. Less people."

"Forget it," I replied. "We're not taking a little girl to a condemned hotel. We should probably get out of here anyway. This isn't really the place for . . ."

"The girl from Florida!" A man wearing khaki shorts and a white T-shirt with underarms stained with in sweat came trotting up the beach in our direction. His face was sunburned, his eyes red and rheumy.

"Hey!" A woman in mirrored sunglasses and a police badge clipped to the waist of her gray slacks stomped in the man's direction. Her black hair was lacquered down onto her scalp and pulled back into bun so severe that it looked more like punishment than a style; her lips were painted a bold shade of matte red.

I ducked my head, hoping the woman wouldn't notice me. It was Mara Lopez. The last time I'd seen her was a year ago, on a night I'd rather forget. She was dressed differently then, in a beat cop uniform rather than in plainclothes.

The sunburned man glanced briefly over his shoulder at the woman and then went on. "The search dogs found her. She was almost completely buried in the sand." He stopped to catch his breath and dab his face with a red and white bandanna that he'd pulled from his back pocket. Whispers of *pobrecita* passed through the crowd.

"Move on, señor!" Mara Lopez roared, dodging the reporter who'd just materialized to shove a microphone in her face. "This is a crime scene. Leave it to the professionals."

"Está muerta?" someone shouted from the crowd.

"Let's go, Celia," Ruben commanded, picking up the bags he'd set down and grabbing his cousin by the arm.

"Sí," the red-faced man lamented with a sad, slow nod. "She was probably in the water for a long time."

"Move it!" Mara Lopez issued her command in English and again in Spanish. "We're trying to do our jobs here." Despite my efforts to hide, her eyes landed on mine. I saw myself— a doubled, distorted reflection—in the lenses of her glasses.

I looked away and noticed that Celia had crouched down and wedged herself between the legs of the people standing in front of us. All ten of her fingers were resting on the police tape, and she'd gone as still as a mountain, her eyes fixed on a cluster of people I assumed were more detectives near the edge of the water. They were examining something at their feet.

"Celia, now!" Ruben demanded.

"Let's go." I picked up Celia, and once in my arms, she wound her legs around my torso and clutched my shoulders. I followed Ruben and Carlos as they wedged themselves through the growing crowd. Together we made our way silently back up to the Avenida.

Eventually, Ruben broke the silence awkwardly: "I forgot eggs."

"We'll have to go back to the market," he added. "Rico's coming over to the house later. You guys can come, too."

The last part of his sentence was nearly drowned out as a cop car hurtled around the corner and screamed past us in the direction of the beach.

"Do you have a sister, Lucas?" Celia asked, as I unwound her limbs from around my body and set her down.

"No. Why?"

Celia didn't get the chance to answer because Ruben took her by the hand and dragged her back toward the market. She did, however, look over her shoulder and wave.

Carlos and I waited until they'd crossed the street and disappeared from sight before hailing a cab to take us back to the old city. During the ride, we both stared out our windows and watched the same line of gray clouds descending from the eastern sky.

"I guess we forgot to tell you. La Lopez got promoted," Carlos eventually said. "She's a detective now."

Last summer, when she was just a beat cop, Mara Lopez—nicknamed La Lopez by the neighborhood kids—hauled me in for underage drinking and drunk and disorderly conduct. According to her, some viejo down on Calle Vecinto called in a tip claiming that a group of kids, included el chico rico (the rich kid: me) were down on the pier, acting all borracho, smashing beer bottles and scaring las turistas.

Most of that was true—though, to my credit, I think the bottle smashing was dramatic flair on the part of the old man—but that doesn't make up for the fact that Rico and Ruben and everyone else on that pier who was stumbling drunk had been sent off with nothing more than a stern warning. I, however, had been hauled down to the San Juan jail by La Lopez herself, where I'd spent the rest of the night in cell with a man in a grease-stained mechanic's uniform who snored like a broken furnace and smelled like rum and bird shit. The next morning, my dad, dressed to the nines as always, came down to pay a "fine" I assumed was generous enough to wipe the charge from my record.

"You need to get a handle on your boy," then Officer Lopez had warned as we were leaving the station, "before he does something he can't buy his way out of."

"*You* need to get a handle on how to run your department," my dad had shot back. "Maybe you should try focusing on bringing in real criminals rather than kids who aren't guilty of anything aside from a momentary lapse in judgment."

But I'd been guilty of more than that, my dad had told me in the car on the way home. I'd been guilty of being the one white kid in a group of otherwise nonwhite kids. According to him, Mara Lopez was just like all the others. Puerto Rico was full of women like her, he said—women with icepick stares who hated the whites and always blamed them for ruining their island and liked to mete out punishment like it was their divine right.

I remember wishing he'd just shut up. He was ranting,

and I had a headache. The car was filled with the spice-musk scent of his Burberry cologne. He'd put on too much this morning, and I was choking on it. The car was also full of his sense of entitlement, which stunk worse than his cologne. At one point, I remember wondering which was worse: being stuck in a town car with my dad or having been stuck in a jail cell with a snoring, stinking mechanic.

What my dad didn't get was that Mara Lopez hated me not because I was white but because I was spoiled. I sometimes hated myself for the same reason.

FIVE

THE SUMMER I turned twelve, a daughter of one of the hotel maids taught me how to kiss. She was older than me, maybe fourteen, but she seemed much older by the way she dressed—in short jean shorts and cropped tank tops—and by the things she said. Nothing ever impressed her, and everything was lame.

For a reason I never figured out, she'd chosen to take me on as a project. Every day for a week she would sneak into my room during the hot hours of the afternoon and sit me down cross-legged on the floor at the foot of my bed. I'd listen carefully to her instructions. She'd point to the hollow between her collarbones and tell me to kiss her there first; she'd point to her bottom lip and tell me to kiss her there next. She'd take my hands and put them on each of her round, smooth shoulders, and she'd tell me to move my fingers up and down her throat. I did exactly as she said. She'd give me tips: slower, less pressure, more pressure, more movement. Sometimes she'd talk about all the other boys she'd let kiss and touch her and she'd compare what I was doing to what they'd done before.

"You're not the best," she once told me. "But you're not the worst either."

She was the first girl to make me hungry and desperate to the point that I would stare up at the ceiling and fantasize about her at night. More than anything I wanted her to think that I was an enthusiastic and capable learner, ready for anything. But mostly she just seemed bored.

One day she came to my room and didn't want to start kissing right away. First, she asked if I'd heard the story of the young nun. I told her I hadn't. She asked if I knew that before this hotel was a hotel, it was a convent. I told her everybody knew that. She asked if I knew that the very room we were sitting in, the room I'd stayed in every year for as long as I could remember had, hundreds of years ago, belonged to a nun who had died.

"The story es muy triste," the girl said.

According to her, the nun was young, around fifteen, and the day before she'd entered the convent, she'd fallen in love with the local butcher's son. Once a week, after saying her morning prayers and washing the floors of the convent with a potato sack, she would sneak out and give the butcher's son letters she'd written in the margins of pages she'd torn from her Bible. At night, after all the nuns were asleep, the butcher's son would jump the walls of the convent and slide his responses under her door.

"They were the best, most romantic love letters you could imagine," the girl said dreamily. "They were about him wanting to lie in bed next to her and run the tips of his fingers across her lips and her neck and stomach and hips. She wrote to him saying that thoughts of them being together and touching each other kept her awake at night. She told him her body was on fire. She begged him to find a way for them to run away to Mayagüez or Ponce, to some place where nobody knew them and they could be together."

"Have you seen the notes?" I remember asking.

I wanted the story to be over so I could put my hands and mouth on the girl's salty skin.

"Of course I haven't seen them." She looked at me like I was an idiot. "How could I've seen them? This happened *way* before I was even born."

According to the girl, the young nun kept the butcher's son's letters folded in the fabric of her habit, so she could pretend that the papers pressing against her bare skin were his hands, but one evening, as she walked across the courtyard on her way to vespers, several of the letters fell out and scattered across the ground. A few blew away in the wind; others landed in the fountain and turned to mush, but an older nun snatched one out of the air. She turned that letter in to the abbess, who was mortified. As punishment, the young nun was locked in her room—*this very* room, the girl who taught me to kiss said—without any food and just a small cup of water. She was told to come out only when she'd purged herself of all desire and was convinced that she was pure of heart.

Two days passed, then five. As they walked by her door, none of the other nuns ever heard their sister calling out to them. They expected those calls; they expected that after many prayers and with knees bruised and sore, that the young nun's heart would've been stripped of all affection for the butcher's son.

After a week, the abbess, with all the other nuns stacked behind her, finally unlocked and opened the door. They found the young nun dead on her bed, her green-gray skin a stark contrast to the now black blood that had spilled from her wrists and dried into her sheets. Scattered around her were the letters from the butcher's son that hadn't blown away, along with loose pages from her Bible. The nuns gasped. Some dropped into dead faints when they realized what their sister had done with the pages of the holy book.

"That's why they put you in this room, you know," the girl told me, "to scare you into leaving. Everyone here hates you and your dad for coming in and acting all stuck up. They're waiting for the young nun to come back and shake you from your sleep and tell you to leave her room."

Then, finally, the girl let me kiss her.

If the girl was trying to scare me, it didn't work. Every

night for the rest of that summer, I stayed awake as long as I could and waited for the nun to come back to her room. I even left notes for her, first on my bedside table, then near the door where she'd know to expect them. In those notes, I told her I wanted to help her. I didn't know how, but I would try.

But those late nights were a waste. The young, triste nun never came, unless it was to look over me as I slept.

By the following summer, the girl who had taught me to kiss was gone. The other maids told me her mother had saved up enough to move to New York.

Over time, the memories of my kissing lessons faded. They came back, however, when I'd found that first note—the one with Marisol's crossed-out wish—slid under my door, and then again, after I came back from Condado Beach and found another.

SIX

LIKE THE ONE with Marisol's crossed-out wish, this note had been written on stationery from the hotel. But unlike the one with Marisol's crossed-out wish, it hadn't been tossed over the wall last night. It had been tossed over the wall five years ago. By me.

I wish I could lift the curse over the house at the end of Calle Sol so the birds would fly over it again.

The paper was dirty and smudged in places, as if passed through many sets of hands, and the crease in the center was fragile, as if it had been unfolded, read, and refolded several times.

And, underneath my barely legible scrawl, in that perfect cursive: *So, what's stopping you?*

"Señor Knight, is there a problem?"

I spun around. Clara, an elderly woman who had been working at the hotel since as long as I could remember, was standing in front of me on the mezzanine, holding a tray from room service. She glanced at my door, which was wide open, and then to the paper in my hand. She smiled slyly.

"It's not what you . . . " I stammered.

"I have your dinner here, Señor Knight," she said, wiping away her grin so quickly I wondered if I'd imagined it.

I shook my head and put my hand to my now-throbbing left temple. "I'm not hungry. Please stop calling me Señor Knight. Just call me Lucas."

"Sí, Señor Knight." Clara nodded and headed over to the staircase. She took a single step down, stopped, and glanced in my direction. That same sly smile flickered and then disappeared. As she descended the stairs, the dishes on her tray rattled against each other.

Hushed voices came from the other side of the courtyard. There, a cluster of housekeepers, all in their humble gray shifts and clunky black shoes, stared at me the way grandmothers do when they know they have age and wisdom on their side, chin tipped up slightly, eyes narrowed.

I crammed the note into my back pocket along with the other and took off down the mezzanine. I leapt down the stairs two at a time, and, after weaving my way through the line of guests checking in at the front desk, burst onto the street.

From there, I sprinted in the direction of the scientist's house.

Once, when I was a kid, I'd made the mistake of repeating to my dad some of the stories I'd heard from the señoras about the house at the end of Calle Sol. It had happened, of course, during breakfast. I remember him neatly folding up the newspaper he'd been reading. After taking a sip of coffee, he'd set his porcelain cup down slowly and leaned across the breakfast table. He'd told me not to believe old ladies. He'd said it was true that the man who lived in the house at the end of Calle Sol *was* a scientist who *did* work out in the forests near Rincón, but that did not mean he was a cruel man whose neglect drove his wife first to madness, then to witchcraft, then, finally, away for good. The windows of the house were shuttered, not to seal in some kind of curse, but because the man was rarely home.

"The women on this island are ignorant, Lucas," my dad had said. "Because they are ignorant, they are fearful, and because they are fearful, they make up stories to explain things that don't need explaining. Ignore them. Don't let their nonsense make you fearful, too."

After that, he'd reached for his newspaper, popped open the pages, and went back to reading.

His advice had missed its mark. The señoras' stories didn't make me fearful; I didn't fear stories, or closed-up houses, or witches, or notes from ghosts, or even the possibility of being cursed. I'd spent my whole life on this island running toward those things, throwing rocks back at those who threw rocks at me, waiting up for phantoms. What I feared was a future where I ended up a version of my dad: oblivious and arrogant, disappointed in clearly beautiful things.

Most everyone in Old San Juan hated my dad because it was easy to hate my dad. He came in and built resorts on their beautiful beaches. He destroyed or warped everything the locals loved about their island in the name of "progress." He talked down to them. When we walked through the public squares, I would watch people sneer at him behind his back. Old women would flick their fingers and mutter curses.

I'd tried to be different, but despite my efforts to not become my dad, it was happening. If people hated him, they hated me, too—they hated the way I always had money but no job, how I was arrested for minor offenses but never charged, how I broke their daughters' hearts and only sort of cared. And if they hated me, they would have no problem trying to scare me. What people never seemed to realize, though, was that I don't scare easy.

Toward the middle of Calle Sol, Señora Garcia came out of her courtyard in her bathrobe bare-handing a rigid, dead cat. It was most likely the latest victim of Señor Guzmán and his glass-laced chicken scraps. If the old woman wondered why I was running full tilt down her street in the middle of the day, she didn't show it. After casting a disinterested glance in my direction, she dropped the cat into the trash can, wiped her hands on her robe, and walked back into her courtyard. I passed her gate just in time to hear the latch click into place.

I neared the end of the street and slowed. The scientist's house looked like it always looked: derelict and unloved except for the leaves bursting over the courtyard wall.

When I got to the gate, I stopped to catch my breath and study a series of rusted-over iron latches affixed to the wood.

Inspired by Marisol's boldness from last night, I glanced up and down the empty street and then pounded my fist against the gate five times.

Within seconds, I heard an interior door open, followed by the sound of slow footsteps across stone, followed by the squeals of metal locks and hinges protesting their use. Overhead, a seagull let out a shrill cry. I looked up to see it gliding in my direction. Just before passing over my head, the bird squawked as if a handful of feathers had been yanked from its skin. Its body twisted violently, and it flew off in the opposite direction.

All the birds knew better than to fly over a cursed house.

"You're Michael Knight's son, are you not?"

I turned my gaze down to the man in front of me and momentarily lost my voice.

I expected the scientist to be some decrepit thing, hunched over and clutching a cane with a hand frozen by arthritis. In my mind, the years of guilt, poison, and pain would've appeared in the lines of a sagging face and cataract-clouded eyes.

Instead, I saw a man roughly my dad's age. He was standing up board-straight, dressed like a rich person from a Dickens novel, with brown herringbone pants, a matching vest, and a white button-up shirt. His only slightly graying hair was long on top and hung across his forehead in unkempt waves. A rose-gold watch chain dangled from his breast pocket.

I glanced over his shoulder and into the courtyard, not knowing who or what else I was expecting to find. My heart beat wildly, so much so that I pressed my hand to my chest.

"Am I correct, young man? You're the junior Michael Knight?"

His voice had traces of an Irish or English accent. The señoras had said he wasn't from the island, and I'd assumed that meant he was from the mainland. His eyes narrowed, belying impatience behind his good manners.

I cleared my throat. "I go by my middle name . . . Lucas."

"How can I help you, Lucas Knight?" His gaze shifted to the street behind me. "Please step in from the rain."

"It's not rain—" A single drop landed on the bridge of my nose. The scientist stepped back and held the gate open.

I took my first uneasy step into a small, strange wilderness.

Tall trees with reedy, rough trunks and green leaves as wide as an open book mingled with squat bushes bearing tiny red berries and five-inch spines that looked as if they could easily spear a human hand. Strands of ivy crept around orange terra-cotta pots, through the gnarled root system of an ancient banyan tree, and up the interior courtyard walls. The ivy also covered the bricked-over ground, creating patches of dense carpet. Some of its vines formed tight corkscrews around stems and tree limbs. They were tiny, determined stranglers. As the rain picked up, the drops bounced off the plants, causing their leaves to start to pulse as if electrified.

The smell in the courtyard wasn't earthy or loamy; instead it was heavy and hot and sharp like rubbing alcohol or the old bottle of grappa my dad kept in his liquor cabinet back home in Houston.

A narrow brick path connected the roughly ten-foot distance from the gate to the entrance of the house proper. Many of the houses in Old San Juan were built this way, with a courtyard surrounding a house, or, like with the St. Lucia, a convent surrounding a courtyard. At the end of the path and just next to the front door of the house was a knee-high pot containing a harmless-looking houseplant, like something I'd once bought from the grocery store to give to my aunt during a hospital stay. I stopped in front of it and leaned forward to examine the splotchy pattern of green and light yellow on its leaves.

"I wouldn't get too close to that if I were you," the scientist said as he passed me. "That's dumb cane." I turned to see him pull out his watch, flip it open, check the time, and then snap it shut. "It's lovely to look at but a bit of an irritant."

He held open the door to his house and gestured for me to enter, which I did. Even though it was lightly raining outside, the entryway I stood in was full of light. The ceiling two stories up was made entirely of glass. There was no reason for the house to ever throw open its windows with the sun shining in from above like that.

"You seem out of breath. I'll fetch you something to drink." The scientist closed the front door, sealing us in. I mumbled my thanks, and then searched the room for any sign of a small, taunting witch.

The decor of the house made it seem as if I'd stepped back in time and across the Atlantic. In a sitting room to my left, dark red curtains were drawn over the tightly shuttered windows. Two leather chairs sat on opposite sides of a brass-topped table. On that table was a chessboard, its black and white pieces frozen mid-battle. On the wall just above a carved mahogany chest hung two long swords in their scabbards, forming a flattened *X*. Rows upon rows of leather-bound books lined shelves that took up two of the three walls. A mahogany desk that matched the style of the chest was wedged in the corner, supporting precarious stacks of books and loose leaves of paper and old copies of *El Nuevo Día*.

The focal point of the room was a large and elaborate candelabra made from stiffly bent iron and reclaimed wood the width and shape of railroad ties. It must have been six feet in diameter and centuries old.

It was all very . . . *masculine*.

"I typically don't receive that many visitors, Mr. Knight," I heard the scientist shout from the kitchen, "so you must excuse the mess. I was just having tea."

I had no idea what he was talking about. Aside from the cluttered desktop, everything was pristine.

"This is quite a house," I called out after clearing my throat. "It looks a lot like the inside of the St. Lucia."

"I've noticed that, yes! Your father and I have similar tastes."

I glanced to my right and into a formal dining room. On the far side of a long banquet table, two glass doors opened onto a side yard. The wind brought in the scent of salt water from the ocean and that same bitter scent from the plants. Next to those glass doors, a staircase with an iron banister curled up to a second floor.

I hadn't noticed the scientist return until he was standing in front of me, holding out a small tumbler of ice water. The fingers wrapped around that glass were long, lean, and built for precision. They looked like they'd done their fair share of studying, folding up, and categorizing small things; they were more than capable of producing a tight, perfect script.

The scientist entered his dining room, where he retrieved a porcelain cup and saucer from a china hutch, and then went over to the far end of the table to pour hot water from a white ceramic pot. Near the pot were a half-filled cup and saucer and a thick, hardback book that had been placed face down to mark its place. Next to that was small plate speckled with leftover crumbs. It was a place setting for one.

"Please excuse my interrupting you, sir," I said, setting down my untouched glass of water so I could take the cup and saucer he was offering me. They were some of the most delicate pieces of porcelain I'd ever held, pure white rimmed with gold.

"That's fine," the scientist replied with a smirk. "How can I help you?"

I took a long drawn-out sip of harsh black tea to buy some time to think. Judging by the fact that he didn't know I went by my middle name and that he was looking at me like I'd just crash-landed into his house from the moon, I doubted he had any idea why I was standing in his dining room politely sipping his brutal tea. Either that or he was skilled at being deceitful.

The scientist tapped his thumb on the rim of his cup and pursed his lips slightly, waiting for me to state the reason for my visit. I went on delaying by pretending to be interested in every small detail of the room. My eyes eventually landed on a frame on one of the walls of the study, which proudly displayed a diploma from Exeter College, Oxford.

There was a lot of calligraphy in what looked like Latin, but underneath all that, in plain, clearly written English: "Rupert Ford, Doctorate of Life Sciences."

Bingo.

"Mr. Knight. Would you care to state your business, or are you just going to stand there all day?"

I looked to the scientist, cleared my throat again, and steeled my nerve. "I was wondering if you could give me some advice."

"Advice?" His right eyebrow cocked up high. He had every reason to be skeptical. I was the very definition of flying by the seat of my pants.

"My dad told me that you were a scientist, Dr. Ford, that you study plants . . . "

He took a sip of tea. "I'm a botanist, yes. As you saw just outside, I have a fondness for rare flora."

"Hmm, yes." I nodded, put on my best pondering-life's-questions face, and continued. "Well, I'm also interested in studying plants, and I was wondering if you had any recommendations of places I could go for college." I laughed lamely, and what I said next was a bad attempt to be humble and charming. "I see you went to Oxford, but I'm thinking that I might have to aim a little lower than that."

Dr. Ford found me neither funny nor charming. His mouth pulled into a frown.

The questions "How's your wife?" and "It is possible that your witch daughter left some notes under my door?" rolled around on my tongue.

The rain outside came down harder, hitting the glass ceiling and producing a sound like muffled applause. Since the doors to the courtyard on the side of the house were open, puddles were beginning to form on the interior tiles.

"Shouldn't you close those?" I asked.

"Mr. Knight." The scientist drew my name out slowly and took a step in my direction. The rain spilling into his house was apparently of no importance. "You show up at my door unannounced to tell me that you're interested in botany and ask me what colleges you might consider attending. Do I understand you correctly?"

"Yes, you do."

I hoped to God Dr. Ford wouldn't start quizzing me on the plant kingdom.

There was another long pause as the scientist continued staring at me with the disarmingly severe eyes of someone who spends his time analyzing living things. Aside from the sound of the rain and the ticking of a distant clock, the house was quiet.

Then there was a sudden twitch in Dr. Ford's left eye. His head snapped in the direction of the courtyard. I followed his gaze and watched an empty terra-cotta pot near the edge of the door tip on its base and then shatter against the brick porch. A thin stream of rainwater dribbled from its mouth.

At that point, the conversation shifted from bad to over.

"I have to leave town this afternoon." Dr. Ford slammed his saucer down on the table and strode across the room to pull the doors shut. As he roughly fastened the latch, the glass panes shook in their sashes. "While I'm gone I'll give your question some thought and get back to you. I might be able to help, as I've somehow managed to maintain a few important connections while quarantined on this godforsaken island."

I knew the breezes weren't strong enough to knock over something that heavy; something (a cat?) or someone (a girl?) had to have tipped it over. As I took a step forward, watching the wind gently push the broken remains of the pot back and forth, like a hand rocking a cradle, Dr. Ford snatched the cup and saucer out of my hand, causing scalding hot liquid to spill across my wrist. I winced, but Dr. Ford either didn't notice or didn't care.

"Is there anything else I can help you with?"

"Not right now, no," I hissed.

"Well, then." Dr. Ford wrapped his long fingers around my upper arm and steered me in the direction of the door. "It was a pleasure, Mr. Knight, but time's wasting. I do have to get ready to be going."

As he practically wrestled me into his foyer, I noticed a small painting on the wall hung up near the front door. It was of a stretch of beach I recognized, out near Rincón. It was where I learned to surf, with its big waves and miles of massive trees. In delicate wisps of greens and blues and oranges, the painter captured the glimmering ocean and swaying treetops.

"I know this beach," I said, grinding to a halt. "It's Rincón. Who painted this?"

"I did." He answered without looking at either the painting or me. "I have a lab there and in my free time I like to paint."

He flung open the door and hustled me down the stone path. With his free hand he yanked his pocket watch from his vest and checked the time. I snuck a glance in the direction of the broken pot; there was nothing near it, aside from several dense shrubs. Dr. Ford pulled open the gate and then waited for me to step through it. We both ignored the fact that we were in the process of getting soaked.

"Is that where you're going today, sir?" I asked. "Out to Rincón?"

He disregarded my question and asked one of his own: "Are you sure, Michael Lucas Knight, that plant science is the branch of study to which you want to commit yourself? I ask because a man can get lonely when he chooses to devote himself to another living thing that isn't capable of giving anything in return." Droplets of rainwater burst off his lips as he spoke. "You'd be wise to keep that in mind."

I stepped onto the sidewalk, turned, and put on my sincerest smile. "I'm committed, Dr. Ford. Plants are my passion. But I appreciate your advice. I really do."

The gate slammed in my face before my last words had even left my mouth.

SEVEN

I CAME IN through the doors of the Hotel St. Lucia as the sun was setting and asked Jorge at the desk if anyone had come in recently looking for me.

"Not that I know of, Señor Lucas."

"What about an older, well-dressed gringo?" I asked.

"You'll have to be more specific than that," he replied, leaning in with a grin. "You are aware of this hotel's star rating, no?"

It was Jorge's cordial way of telling me that I'd just asked a really stupid question. Older, well-dressed gringos were pretty much par for the course around here.

"What about a little girl with green skin?"

The grin on Jorge's face remained, but his eyes flickered with confusion.

"Little girl? Green skin, green hair?"

I was being a brat, harassing Jorge in the lobby of a

five-star hotel with water dripping off my clothes onto a checkerboard marble tile floor that cost more than some people make in a lifetime. But I couldn't help it. The events of the day had left me . . . *unhinged*.

"Piel verde?" I asked. "Pelo verde?"

Jorge's grin vanished. He opened his mouth but didn't get the chance to respond because my dad chose that precise moment to saunter into the lobby. He glanced at the puddles forming on his marble floor and frowned. He didn't ask where I'd been, and I didn't tell him.

"You're making a mess," he said.

"I'm not going to Rincón."

My dad shrugged and waited for Jorge to come around the desk and escort him out with an open umbrella so he wouldn't have to suffer the indignity of getting wet on the way to his waiting town car.

I trudged up to my room, grateful there wasn't a third note waiting for me when I opened the door, but also disappointed there wasn't a message from Marisol—not that she'd promised to leave one. After I showered and changed into dry clothes, I remembered how Ruben said earlier that he and Rico would be hanging out at his house. If I hurried there would still be beer.

But by the time I got to Ruben's, he and Rico were in the process of polishing off their second six-pack. They were sitting next to one another on the floor at the foot of Ruben's bed, watching a documentary about Geronimo on the public television station. Both of them were red-eyed and half asleep. They were probably stoned.

I scanned the room for an unopened beer, but all I saw were crushed cans.

"What the hell?" I asked, kicking what I thought was an empty. A thin stream of white foam poured out from the mouth of the can and onto the rug.

"I got here as fast as I could," I added.

"Not fast enough, apparently." Rico reached up to absently tug on the dime-sized St. Anthony medallion that always hung around his neck.

"Where's Marisol?" I asked.

Ruben peered up at me, took another swig from the Medalla in his hand, and laughed.

"Have you looked at yourself in the mirror today, man?" he asked. "You look terrible—all twitchy and shit. What, are you getting sick or something?" He glanced over at Rico, but Rico wasn't paying attention. "Not that we have anything else to drink, but if we did, I'd highly recommend taking a break for a while, eh? Get some sleep."

I grimaced. "What are you, my mother?"

Ruben laughed again, and as he did, his gut bounced lightly under his shirt.

"Hell no, Lucas," he said. "Everybody knows you don't have a mother."

Something, like the thinnest of twigs, snapped in my brain. Within the same second, I'd kicked the beer can out of Ruben's hand with my right foot and then shoved my knee into his throat. He made sad gurgling sounds as piss-yellow liquid seeped out from between his lips and his hands clutched at the fabric of my jeans.

"I'm sorry," I snarled through a jaw clenched tight. "What did you just say?"

"Luke!" His words were garbled, probably because I was crushing his windpipe. "What the hell is wrong with you? Shit! Rico, man, help me out!"

Rico gave Ruben and me an apathetic once-over. His eyes then went back to the television and the mean-looking Apache with the gun.

"You're on your own, Ruben," he said. "You know better than to talk about a man's mother."

"I'm sorry, okay?" Ruben's words continued to struggle to find their way out. "Now get off me!"

The instant I backed away, Ruben sprang up and threw me against the door. I caught myself with one of my hands, launched off the door, and shoved him back, causing him to fall, trip over his feet, and crash into the side of his bed. As he stood up and straightened his shirt, he stared me down, mumbling curses under his breath.

My next words were directed to Rico. "Where are the girls? Are they coming over or what?"

Rico dropped his medallion and looked over his shoulder

at me. "I don't know where they are, okay? Ruth called earlier and said that she was waiting for Marisol to get to her place. That was around seven, maybe."

I glanced at the clock on Ruben's nightstand. It was eight forty-eight.

The last thing I wanted to do was hang around with two guys who were drunk and stoned while I was neither.

"I'm leaving. You two have fun." I turned to go but stopped, scraping my fingernails through my hair. "Hey," I said. "Do you two remember any stories about the house on the end of Calle Sol?"

Ruben continued with his indignant scowling while Rico stared at me blank-faced.

"We would make up stories about it being cursed," I urged.

Rico looked down and shrugged. His fingers flew back to his medallion.

"I don't remember any stories like *that*," Ruben said, wiping foam off his chin with his shirtsleeve. "I do remember a story about a nun who hung herself in your hotel back when it was a convent. You seeing ghosts, Lucas?" Ruben continued to shout after me as I turned and started down the hall. "Is that why you look so bad? Serves you right! You are such an asshole. You know that, don't you?"

I knew that, yeah.

I reached the bottom of the stairs and passed through the kitchen where Celia was sitting by herself at the table playing with an assembly of plastic, pink-skinned dolls. She was stroking their hair while speaking to them in a language only they could understand, all babbles and shushes, like water in a cold stream.

Once outside, I hailed a cab and told the driver to take me to Condado Beach.

Other than the stray strips of police tape flapping in the wind and a small cluster of pillar candles—the kind with the pictures of the saints on them—the beach was empty. There were no cops, no curious onlookers, certainly no tourists. When families plan their trips to paradise, they don't exactly expect a dead girl to wash up right in front of their hotel. My dad didn't own any of the high-rises in this part of San Juan, but if he had, he'd be in full-on damage control mode right now, easing anxieties with smooth talk, complimentary trips to the spa, and meal vouchers.

Unlike the señoras with their elephant memories, however, the tourists from the mainland never let something as unpleasant as a dead girl dim their days for very long. Most likely by tomorrow morning the beach would be packed again, and everyone would be back to fun in the sun.

For now, it was good to be alone. I took off my shoes and made my way down the wet sand toward La Andalusia. Its name, spelled out in huge, curving red letters that hadn't been lit up for decades, faced the water and reminded me of a lighthouse with a negligent keeper. I snaked around the side of the hotel to where one of several first-story windows was boarded over with a thin square of plywood. This had always been my way in. The nails holding the square in place had rusted to the point of being useless, and the plywood came off easily. I ducked through the frame and landed inside what used to be a ballroom. A cobwebbed crystal chandelier hung from the ceiling above a pile of chairs upholstered in red-and-gold-striped fabric. The once-vibrant colors were now muted by dust. Wooden tables were stacked on top of each other, some with canvas tarps hanging off them. A long, curving bar took up the length of one wall. Behind it were dirty mirrors that hadn't given a reflection of anyone in a very long time. Scattered across the water-stained carpet were small leaves, brown and crisp. There were empty bags of Fritos and cans of Coke, proof of my previous visits. The wind whistled from invisible cracks in hidden places and caused the walls of the empty building to shake. The entire place smelled like mildew.

Several summers ago, Rico, Carlos, Ruben, and I first snuck into this high-rise to chase each other through the hallways and up and down stairwells. We played bartender, and when that got old, went into the kitchen and trashed it. During one of our games of hide-and-seek, I'd stayed in a storage closet on the twelfth floor for over two hours until Rico found me. As I was nestled between the shelves, I remember thinking that this huge, empty hotel was where I wanted to live for the rest of my life.

Since then, I'd snuck in countless times, sometimes with my friends, but usually alone. I loved this building because it didn't have any stories about curses or magic attached to it. All its noises could be attributed to wind or to an old foundation settling in the sand or to rats, but never to ghosts. La Andalusia was a giant empty vessel: all mine. I could find clarity here.

I stood in front of one of the non-boarded-up windows for a while, watching the slanting rain pelt the ocean. Eventually, I dragged a rust-red sofa into the middle of the large room and collapsed onto it. I fell asleep there, listening to the hiss of wind. When I woke, it was still dark. The rain had stopped, but drops speckled the windows.

Sure enough, the silent solitude of La Andalusia worked. With sleep came a plan.

I sat up, pulled the two wishes from my pocket, and grinned. Part of what had contributed to my funk was the fact that I'd have to wait until Dr. Ford came back from his trip to Rincón in order to get some answers about these notes. But, I now realized, that didn't have to be the case. I'd already broken into one place today—this one—so what was the harm in doing it again?

Because of the rain, the beach was a mess of fallen coconuts and palm fronds torn from their trees. Most of the hotel rooms were either completely dark or had their curtains drawn. I didn't know how late it was, but I hoped there would be a taxi at the nearest hotel stand so I wouldn't have to wait for one of the bellmen to call me one.

It's wise to tiptoe along on a dark beach. I should've been keeping my eyes on the sand, watching for the shimmer of a broken piece of glass so I wouldn't accidently slice my foot open.

But I was running barefoot—away from the shoreline and toward the dunes—when I tripped over a log and fell face-first to the ground. I cursed, flipped myself over, spit the sand from my mouth, and reached down to try and free one of my feet that had gotten tangled in seaweed.

That's when I realized that what was wrapped around my toes wasn't seaweed. It was dark hair matted into ropey tangles. What I'd tripped over wasn't a log. It was a girl. Her eyes were milk-white, speckled with sand, and staring up at the moon. Her blue and bloated lips were parted and pulled back from her teeth into a wicked grimace. The gold *M* around her neck glinted in the moonlight.

PART TWO

ISABEL

EIGHT

THE POLICE SAID it was a drowning. Marisol had been in the water for at least twenty-four hours and had washed up after the rainstorm. That's why she had so many small cuts all over her skin. They were nips from curious fishes and scratches from bumping up against hunks of wood and flotsam as she was tossed around by the chop.

I was taken to the station and ushered into a room with concrete walls. I was questioned, given a cup of weak coffee to lessen the shock, made to wait, questioned again by a second person, then by a third. After another cup of coffee and another delay, Mara Lopez entered the room. By then I was half delirious. The caffeine on an empty stomach had given me the shakes. I told La Lopez I wanted to go home. She put her hand on my knee, gave it a *there, there* kind of pat. She told me she just wanted to make sure she had the details right: why I was alone on a beach at four in the morning, in what capacity I knew Marisol, those types of things. I answered honestly; I had nothing to hide.

She also said she'd called my dad out in Rincón and explained the situation to him. He told her to relay a message: *We'll talk when I get back.*

"His son tripping over a dead Puerto Rican girl in the middle of the night apparently isn't enough to pull him away from his business," she added.

It was mid-morning when I was finally allowed leave. I went to Ruben's house, where I found Marisol's mother sitting on the couch in the hothouse living room—all the doors and shutters were closed as a sign of mourning. The air inside was thick with the smell of smoke and incense. I handed her some lilies I'd bought from the market and offered my condolences. It didn't really matter what I gave her or what I said, though. The woman didn't hear a word. Her gaze was locked on the tiny flame of a pillar candle that sat on the coffee table. Her fingers skillfully worked the pink plastic beads of a cheap rosary.

Ruben was self-exiled behind his locked bedroom door upstairs, so for close to four hours, I sat on the couch wedged between Marisol's mom and Marisol's ancient, mute grandmother. I stayed there, sweating, through the duration of many candles, listening to the hiss of the paper fan Ruben's abuela used to keep the mosquitoes at bay and to the clacks of her dentures shifting in her mouth as her lips moved in silent prayer.

All that time did not pass slowly, though. My thoughts ran on a loop: Marisol alive, laughing and determined to jump into the courtyard of the house at the end of Calle Sol; Marisol dead, her twisted limbs coated in wet sand and wrapped in seaweed; Marisol alive, moaning softly as my fingers traced her skin; Marisol dead, her mouth gaped open and her tongue, doubled in size and black.

I finally got up for a drink of water, and there in the kitchen was Celia, standing on a step stool at the counter. She was glaring at a half-cut-up pineapple and sucking on the pointer finger of her left hand. A ten-inch chef's knife sat atop a cutting board. Both it and the pineapple were spotted with blood.

I bolted toward her, but she quickly pulled her finger from her mouth and held it up. The cut wasn't bleeding anymore and not at all deep, just a shallow groove across her skin.

"It slipped." Celia sniffled and then wiped her eyes with the sleeve of her green pajama top. "I'm sorry. I was hungry."

"You shouldn't have done this yourself," I said. "You could've been hurt."

I grabbed the knife, rinsed it with hot water, and tried to salvage some of the fruit.

"The police told us Mari drowned," Celia blurted out, "but I don't understand, because she knows how to swim. She was the one who was trying to teach *me*."

The knife clanged loudly as I slammed it against the counter.

Celia was next to me, still up on her step stool, and when I turned to face her, I was reminded how much she resembled her sister: heart-shaped face, brown eyes that seemed to take in the smallest of details, hair the color of coffee. It was impossible not to picture that hair in wet knots or her cheeks covered in tiny marks left by teething fish.

I was at a loss. I didn't know how to break this to a little girl: sometimes unfair and illogical things happen, and those things have the ability to convince you fairness and logic are illusions, as real as wishes blown off dandelions.

That's when I remembered I had something real and concrete I could give her, even if it wasn't what, who, she really wanted.

"Here." I wiped a sticky hand on my jeans and reached into my pocket. "I got you a present." I pulled out the wolf charm I'd bought for Marisol and pushed it into Celia's small palm. "You're supposed to string it on a necklace, but you can just keep it with you until you can find a chain."

"You got this for *me*?"

I adopted the confident tone and straight-spined posture of someone who wouldn't be so shameless as to lie to a child. "Of course."

"Why?"

I paused, scrambling for an answer. I'd bought the charm for Marisol as a token representing her big plans for the future, but now that the charm was Celia's, it had to mean something different.

"It's a reminder for you to be brave," I replied, "like a wolf."

Celia pinched the charm between her thumb and index finger and examined its hard details. I couldn't tell if she believed me. Even so young, she seemed more naturally skeptical than her sister.

"I'm going upstairs to check on Ruben, alright?" I said, clearing my throat and backing away. "Promise me you won't handle the knife again. I don't want you to get hurt."

Celia turned to watch me go. "I promise." The absent way she said it made me wonder if *I* could believe *her*.

I stood in front of Ruben's closed door and listened to the muffled chatter of his television for a second before knocking and calling out his name. His reply was to tell me to get the hell away from his house—that no one needed my sympathy and that my being there was making everything worse.

I was on my way back to the staircase when I heard a woman's voice—clear like crystal—coming from the television inside Ruben's room.

" . . . newly released details reveal connections between the cases of Sara Fikes and Marisol Reyes . . . "

I slammed the heel of my palm against the door. "Ruben! Let me in! I need to hear this!"

"Are you deaf?" Ruben bellowed. "I said go away."

I pressed my ear against the wood. All I could hear were inaudible clicks and murmurs. Then, more plainly: " . . . go

83

now to Detective Mara Lopez, of the San Juan Police Department, who has been overseeing both investigations."

"Ruben!" I beat the door again. "What are they saying?"

After being met with silence, I grabbed the doorknob with both my hands and shook it. No use. I hit the door again, determined not to stop until Ruben opened it. Finally, he did. Like it had been downstairs, the air in his room was stale, full of the stink of breath.

"*What* is your problem?" he barked. "We're trying to mourn here!"

My eyes only landed on his face for a second, and I supposed he was grateful for that. It was obvious he'd been crying. His eyelids were swollen; pink streaks and splotches marred his cheeks.

Ruben repeated his question, but by then I'd shifted my focus to the television. Detective Lopez had evidently just been asked a question, and her thin, red-painted lips were a tight line as she tried to formulate the appropriate response.

"Both of their bodies were found in the same general area," she said into the cluster of microphones positioned in front of her face, "and they were in roughly the same physical condition."

"Can you describe that condition, detective?" asked someone off camera.

Mara Lopez sighed, not out of impatience, but because she must have anticipated that what she was going to say next might be difficult for some people to hear.

"For the most part their conditions are consistent with what we see from drowning victims here in the tropics. The temperature and saline content of the water along with the plant and marine life tend to leave fairly typical . . . " She paused to find the right word, ". . . traces on the body."

I again pictured Marisol: blue, bloated, tangled in seaweed, the skin of her lips torn like bits of thin paper. My stomach pitched.

"I'm not watching this anymore." Ruben punched the television's power button and then spun around to shove me hard in the chest. "Now get out, Luke!"

I hesitated, but in the end, didn't fight back. It wasn't worth it. I couldn't stand to be in that house anymore anyway.

Back at the hotel, I skipped dinner and instead pilfered a couple of bottles of wine from my dad's stash to take up to my room, where I was determined to drink until I blacked out. But when I stepped through the door, my foot landed directly on a textured cream-colored card.

I snatched it off the ground and immediately recognized the handwriting.

Please come back, it read. *My name is Isabel. I'd like to talk to you about the disappeared girl.*

NINE

THE FRONT GATE of the scientist's house wasn't an option. I grabbed on to it and shook, but its network of locks held it firmly in place.

If forced to guess, I'd have to say the wall surrounding the courtyard was about seven feet tall. No sweat. If I took a running start, I could plant my foot on the wall, push off, and use the momentum to hoist myself over.

I stepped across Calle Sol and looked around to make sure I was alone. If I was Catholic, I would've crossed myself like the señoras do when they need a little extra help from the man upstairs—touching the middle finger of their right hands to their forehead, heart, left shoulder, right shoulder. Since I'm not, I steadied myself with a breath and then shot across the street in five long strides. When the sole of my sneaker hit the wall, it immediately lost traction, causing the entire right side of my face to slam into plaster-covered concrete. I lamely tried to catch myself with my open palms, but went down hard.

I swallowed a string of curses, peeled myself off the ground, wiped the bits of blue plaster off my hands, and went across the street to prepare for another running start. Again, I crossed in five even strides. The sole of my shoe hit the wall—this time it stuck. Momentum carried me a few precious inches, and I was able to grab on to the top of the wall with both hands. From there, I pulled myself up and managed to swing my right leg over the edge.

For a second, I straddled the top of the wall, catching my breath and surveying the dark courtyard and the small, weird forest it contained. After a moment teetering between two worlds, I swung my left leg over and dropped into the garden. The bottoms of my sneakers met slick bricks, and I lost my balance. The last thing I heard before my head hit the ground and I blacked out was a shout that may or may not have come out of my own mouth.

I woke up to a dizzying blur of green leaves and dark sky. Scattered drops of rain were falling into my open mouth and onto my dry lips. Above me, the indistinct figure of a small person came into view, a veil of black surrounding a face. The person, a girl, was saying something; it sounded like she was shouting at me through water.

I was being moved. I could feel my skin scraping against

stone. After mumbling something about a butcher's son and love letters, I blacked out again.

I woke for the second time to the sound of a wasp buzzing in my ear. My eyes snapped wide open, took in the bright moon above, and slammed back shut. I brushed my hand up against my ear, but the buzzing didn't go away.

I remembered: jumping, falling through the leaves, the feeling of being dragged across something hot and hard. My forearms itched. I held them up to my eyes. It looked like the skin on both was covered in blisters.

A girl said, "You're awake. I was starting to get worried."

I craned my head in the direction of the voice. That slight movement hurt, *bad*.

"Who . . . ?" Just the act of forming a word was painful. My peripheral vision was filled with leaves, and they seemed to sway in slow motion, like the tentacles of a giant sea creature.

The girl leaned over me, and the dark and wavy tips of her hair nearly grazed my face. "What was that you said earlier about a butcher?"

"A butcher's *son*," I slurred.

"A *what*?"

"I . . . I'm sorry." I dragged one of my palms across my eyes to try and push the pain out of my head. It didn't work. "I thought you were a nun."

"You know," she said after a pause, "I've never thought of

it that way. You're sort of right, though. I am a nun. And this is my convent Welcome. Finally."

Slowly and with my head still spinning, I stood. I blinked— one, two, three times—and the girl finally came into focus. She didn't have green skin and grass for hair. She was around my age, but bird-boned and short, dressed in jeans that were patched in places and rolled up to her ankles. The hood of the blue long-sleeved sweatshirt she was wearing was thrown over her head in a way that made her look fierce, like a cruiserweight primed for a boxing match.

Prune-purple rings circled her near-black eyes; her brow was furrowed like someone who'd spent her entire life anticipating a fight.

I wasn't feeling like much of an opponent right then. Too much was still out of focus.

My forearm itched like crazy, so I scratched it. This was, apparently, was not the right thing to do.

"Don't do that!" One of the girl's hands flew in my direction.

I kept scratching.

"Those types of rashes have a tendency to spread," she said, cringing. "Just leave it be. You'll be fine in a few hours."

I stopped to hold my arms up to my eyes so I could study the tiny white dots on my skin by the light of the moon. The dots squirmed like maggots. I blinked; they stopped.

"You landed in the plants," the girl said. "I had to move you away from them."

I dropped my arms and peered at the girl in front of me who still seemed less like a solid person and more like a dark, nebulous mass.

The only thing I could do was state the obvious: "They're poisonous. They cause hallucinations. I heard they killed a kitten."

"My dad's a scientist. He studies plants." She smirked. "You have similar aspirations, yeah?"

Her accent was strange: partially British or Irish like that of the scientist, but also suggesting that she'd spent a lot of time on the island. There were hints of Spanish in the rhythm of her words and the way she rounded her vowels.

I ignored her dig and cast a glance through the open glass doors of the house that led to the lit dining room I'd stood in the previous day. My eyes moved to a corner of the court-yard, where a white hammock was strung up near a mas-sive pile of water-logged hardback books and the remains of a single smashed terra-cotta pot. The gold lettering on the spines of the books shimmered; squinting, I tried to make out the author. Borges, probably. It wouldn't have surprised me. It also wouldn't have surprised me if a red and green macaw flew out of the plants, landed on my shoulder, and starting reciting poetry or some shit.

A thin wisp of clarity filtered through my brain long enough for me to remember why I'd launched myself into this bizarre situation. I reached into my back pocket and pulled out the notes.

"What is this?" I asked, holding the slips of paper between us. "How do you know my name?"

The girl tilted her head as if she'd misheard me. "Everyone knows your name."

"Not everyone knows what room I stay in."

"Yes, they do. It's the haunted one."

I focused on the girl's eyes, which now appeared so black that they reminded me of the shiny jet stones of a brooch my mother had worn to my grandmother's—my dad's mother's— funeral. She'd referred to it as her "mourning jewelry."

The girl—Isabel, I now remembered the note had said— was examining me, too, and I could tell by the way her lips were pursed that she wasn't completely convinced she liked what she saw.

I flicked at her last note. "Why did you call her this?"

"Call her what?"

"The disappeared girl."

"I overheard the señora next door say that." Isabel still hadn't taken her eyes from mine. "She was talking to one of our neighbors about a girl named Marisol. She said she'd gone missing and that a boy named Lucas found her on the beach."

"How do you know I know a girl named Marisol?"

"Because the other night I heard the two of you joking about trying to jump over the wall of my house." She paused for a beat. "My *cursed* house."

I choked out a laugh.

"You're kidding, right? How about on the night *before* Marisol and I were *joking* outside your house, you pelted me in the face with rocks?"

Isabel finally broke eye contact. Her thin lips twisted into a sneer as she reached up to tug at the hood of her sweatshirt.

"You were bothering me," she muttered.

"*Bothering* you? This is why you asked me to come here? To rub salt in my wounds and tell me that I've been *bothering* you?"

"It's not like you're the first couple to ever go down there." Isabel threw out her hand, gesturing toward the stone wall on the far end of the courtyard. "I'm tired of being subjected to everyone's amorous encounters. I . . . "

Her mouth slammed shut as if she were trying to catch whatever words were going to fall out of it next, but it wouldn't have mattered because she'd pretty much already landed hard onto my wrong side.

Isabel thought for a moment and changed her course. "I'm sorry. Okay? I wanted you to come so I could apologize. I was playing tricks before—with the other letters, and the stones. I realize now it was all in such poor taste, considering all that's happened to you recently."

"All that's happened," I echoed. "Marisol is *dead*."

It was the first time I'd said those words out loud. In the next instant, my left temple burst with pain, and white light flooded my vision. I had to slam my eyes shut and press my fingers hard into my forehead just to keep my balance.

"You're not well," I heard Isabel say.

"I'm fine," I lied. "But if you wanted to apologize, there are better ways. You could have just written *I'm sorry* on one of your cards. You could have knocked on my door. You didn't have to formally request my presence and make me dive in here like an idiot."

"It's not that simple, actually."

The pain in my head eased enough so that I could peer at Isabel through narrowed eyes. She'd retreated away from me, dissolving herself into the shadows cast off by a canopy of leaves.

She was clearly so strange. All this time cooped up in this house had really taken a toll on her ability to act like a normal human being.

"Why are you hiding?"

She paused and threw her shoulders back. "I'm not."

What a terrible liar Isabel Ford was. Even with my head throbbing and thoughts turning about as smoothly as rusted-over gears, I could see she was trying to give off a casual confidence through the feigned conviction in her stance and in her voice. I'd just done almost the exact same thing at Ruben's house with Celia.

"This is the second time I've come here and made a fool of myself because of you."

She didn't respond, so I went on. "You knocked over that pot yesterday, right?"

Still, silence.

"*Right?*"

Her reply was maddeningly simple: a shrug and an uptick of her chin that meant yes.

"What for?"

Isabel scowled; her brief façade of cool confidence fractured. She ran a hand roughly across her cheek and her chin. It may have been a trick of the light or my unreliable vision, but her nail beds appeared black, as if her fingers had been recently slammed in a car door.

"Like I said, it was a gag. Just a stupid prank. I didn't think you'd actually come."

Again: an obvious lie, but she didn't leave any time for me to point it out before she went on.

"I needed to get *you*." Her first finger emerged from the cuff of her sweatshirt to point at me. "To come *here*." She pointed at her feet. "Leaving the house for long stretches of time is not in my best interest. I'm sick. That's why I . . . *hide*."

"So, you're contagious?"

She frowned. "That's not the way I'd describe my condition, no."

"How would you describe your *condition* then?"

Isabel didn't respond. Instead, her eyes landed on my arms, which were burning from my wrists to the creases of my elbows, and then traveled to the plants around us that pulsed as if held together by a singular heart. A wasp, possibly the same one that had been buzzing around my ear earlier, dipped and weaved in between where she and I were standing. When it flew roughly an inch from her face, Isabel turned her chin slightly in its direction. She blew out as if extinguishing a candle flame. For a split-second the wasp hovered in the air. Then it dropped dead to the ground.

TEN

I DON'T KNOW how many seconds I watched that wasp lie motionless on the bricks. But I do know I said something small and meek—like, *oh*—before I tripped over my own feet to get to the front gate and start to fumble with the latches. A splinter wedged itself underneath my middle fingernail, and I swallowed that new burst of pain. My skin was crawling, and my fingers were trembling to the point that I wanted to tear my useless arms from my shoulders.

"I really am sorry about that rash," I heard Isabel call out from behind me. "The itch should fade in a little while, and any blisters should heal by morning."

I pretended that I didn't hear her. After several desperate seconds, I triumphed over the latches, scrambled through the gate, and then slammed it shut behind me. I'd made it only a few houses down Calle Sol before pain gripped my head again. I braced myself against the cement wall of Señora Garcia's courtyard. Soon, something light and cool began to fall on my arms and the back of my neck. It had started drizzling again, thank God,

By some miracle, I made it back to my room without throwing up in the middle of the street. Once there, I stripped my sweat-soaked shirt off, ran into the bathroom, and turned on the tap. I stuck my face under the running water and took a series of large, desperate gulps. Once I'd had my fill, I let the cold water run over the inflamed skin of my arms and gasped with relief.

As the water ran, I checked my face in the mirror. I looked like shit. My eyes were bloodshot; the strands of my hair had formed into greasy tangles, and despite all I'd just drunk, my lips were dry and cracking.

There was a new loop going through my head: Isabel told me she was sick. There was a wasp. It was alive. She blew on it. It died. I panicked. Isabel told me she was sick . . .

My arms went numb from the cold. I turned off the tap, threw a couple of aspirin down my throat, went into my room, and fell onto my bed.

I must have left the television on earlier because I could hear it buzzing in the background. The meteorologist was talking about the oncoming storm. I peeked to see her pointing at a map of the Atlantic, trying to predict the trajectory of a giant yellow swirl.

Almost immediately, the room started to spin along with the storm. I buried my face into the sheets and squeezed my eyes shut. That was how I managed to force myself to sleep.

97

I woke up late the next morning to the sound of someone banging on my door. Before I opened it, I looked down at my forearms. The bumps were gone, and I wondered if I'd imagined them there in the first place. All that remained, along with a faint itch, were pink blotches, like uneven stripes around both wrists.

Isabel told me she was sick. There was a wasp. It was alive. She blew on it. It died. I panicked. Isabel told me she was sick...

"Lucas!"

I finally flung the door open, and there was Rico, bleary-eyed and frantic.

Behind him the sky was swirling into a thick, dark cream. It was gray, yet it glowed. A cool wind whipped through the courtyard, causing the leaves of the palm trees to slap against each other. There was no rain, not yet, but there would be soon.

The first drops would hit full and fat. The gray sky would burst orange, and the birds would abandon their nests on beaches. Once the winds picked up, the raindrops would fly in needles cutting sideways through the sky.

It was hurricane weather.

Rico saw where my gaze was directed and turned his head. "It's nothing," he said. "Just some cat 3. It'll probably pass to the south and maybe hit Ponce later this afternoon."

Irene had only been a category 1, but I'll never forget the faint *click-tap* when the power went out in the hotel, and how for hours all I could hear was the wail of the storm sirens and the roaring wind. There was a point when that wind shook the glass of the patio doors to my room so violently they shattered. My cheek is still marked with a faint scar from a shard of glass that flew across it. That morning, I had run to my dad's room, watching the palm trees in the courtyard struggle to stay rooted and fighting a wild wind determined to either knock me flat or suck me into the sky.

After the storm had passed everything was quiet. Wet palm fronds ripped from their trees were on everything: cars, roofs, sidewalks, power lines. The stray cats were hiding and didn't come out for days. One person died. He was probably a surfer; they never heeded warnings. Other than that, the old walled city survived to open its windows to the sea again, like it had done hundreds of times before.

"Lucas, listen," Rico said, shoving me on the shoulder and snapping me out of the memory. "Celia's gone."

I blinked. "What?"

"Celia," he repeated. "She wasn't in her bed this morning. Her family thinks she wandered off to search for Marisol. Ruben said she went a little nuts last night, kept asking everyone why they weren't trying to find her. They called the cops, but until the storm comes I'm taking my scooter out to see if I can find her. Maybe you can take one of your dad's cars?"

I nodded but knew it wasn't a possibility. What I *could* do was slip a taxi driver a few twenties and tell him to drive me around for a while.

After throwing on some clean clothes, I flew from my room, down the stairs, and out the front door to hail a cab from the stand across the street from the hotel. Rico could handle the narrower cobbled streets of Old San Juan by himself on his scooter, so I had the driver take me a couple of miles out so I could work from the outlying districts back into the city center.

The sky was darkening, growing more hateful by the second, and the rain was falling down in sheets. People were leaning out windows, snapping their shutters closed, preparing to stay in and brace for the onslaught.

My cab was only about a mile and a half away from the convent when the driver stopped and told me I was out of luck.

"La tormenta!" he said, leaning forward to knock his knuckles on the windshield.

I pulled out all the cash I had and urged him on, telling him in broken Spanish that he was used to driving in the rain, that it rained todos los días here. I needed to find a little girl, una chica desaparecida, didn't he understand?

He didn't, apparently.

I climbed out of the cab. The wind instantly clung to the folds of my wet clothes and tried to pull me both off and to the ground. Trudging down the street, I passed shuttered buildings and pictured the people inside them. On the off chance they had power, they might be wrestling with rabbit-ear antennas, struggling to get TV reception. If they didn't have power, they were likely playing cards or dominoes by candlelight around the dining room table.

It was crazy to be out—a total gringo move. I had to get back to the hotel.

I'd just slogged around a corner when I saw her, through the slanting rain: only a slice of yellow at the far end of an alley, but that was enough. That yellow belonged to a dress I'd run my fingers across, gripped, and pulled at.

"Marisol!" The storm swallowed my cry.

Despite the dark water swirling around my ankles and the persistent winds beating me down, I pulled myself down the alley in her direction. Ten feet ahead, the butter-colored fabric of Marisol's dress fluttered once more, and I watched it, along with the heel of one of her bare feet, vanish around a corner.

I pushed forward, and seconds later emerged from the alley into the empty Plaza de Armas. On a normal day, it would be full of locals going about their lives and tourists posing for pictures. Now, the only vaguely human figures around were the four gleaming white statues—one representing each season of the year—that guarded its central fountain. On the opposite side of the plaza from where I was standing, a dim yellow floodlight appeared to blink as the rain came down in front of it. The twitching fabric of a dress was an illusion caused by water and light.

Grief was a strange thing, bewitching and bewildering. It had convinced both Celia and I that we could defeat a hurricane and track down a phantom.

My muscles were shot, torn and trembling. The wind was hitting my head so hard, I couldn't think. It was time to go home. I leaned into the wind and began to march through the ankle-deep water. When I reached edge of the plaza, I turned. Just to make sure. It was still empty; the yellow floodlight still blinked.

ELEVEN

NO NEW NOTE was waiting for me when I returned to the convent, thank God. I wasn't in any condition—physical or mental—to deal with that right then, but I hadn't even closed my door before my dad rushed up.

"Lucas?" He braced himself against the frame of my open door as he looked me up and down, seeing for the second time in as many days that I was drenched. "I wanted to make sure you were alright. I checked earlier, but you weren't here."

"I got caught in the storm." I wiped the water from my eyes. "It took me a while to get back."

I diverted my gaze from his and noticed that even while riding out a major meteorological event, my dad was dressed to impress. The creases in his suit pants were sharp, and his shirt collar was perfectly starched. Even the brown leather of his shoes shone.

"I left you a message saying I'd come back early and to check in with me. Did you not get it?"

Before I could answer, wind and spray tore through the courtyard, causing my dad to check his balance.

"I didn't get it." I latched on to my dad's arm to steady him. "I just got back."

"Yes, you mentioned that," he replied without looking me in the eye. "I was worried about you. Tell you what—why don't you change into some dry clothes then and have dinner with me? I'll order food and tell you about all you missed in Rincón."

I gathered that last bit was an attempt at a joke, so I forced a smile as I tried to come up with a reason to refuse his invitation. Aside from our breakfasts, we rarely spent time together; he was either holed up in his room on the phone or out on the road. The fact that he'd practically been waiting at my doorstep meant he'd been genuinely worried.

"Luke?"

"Sure," I said, snapping to. "I'll be there in a minute. You didn't get a message, did you? About Celia Reyes?"

My dad shook his head. "No. Is this a friend of yours?"

She's a child! She's missing! How could he have not heard about this?

I changed clothes, shoved my collection of notes into the back pocket of a dry pair of jeans, and fought the wind around the mezzanine to my dad's room. As if this was any other early evening, he was enjoying a glass of red wine. He'd also set the television to the cable channel that plays classical music and was picking from various plates containing cheese, fruit, tiny fried smelts, and a Spanish potato omelet. I sat down and forced myself to eat, even though I wasn't hungry. Under the table my knee bounced uncontrollably as I thought of Celia somewhere out in this weather.

As the rain and branches of trees pummeled the windows, I half-listened while my dad told me about his plan to build a massive Italian villa–style resort on the hills overlooking the beach in Rincón. His firm had already bought the land, and he'd gone out there to meet with the architects and engineers who'd design and construct the place. He envisioned luxury bungalows, a world-class spa, and a series of sparkling wading pools with elaborate fountains made from Venetian marble.

I envisioned a giant blot on a perfect stretch of beach.

"Doesn't that seem excessive?" I asked.

My dad peered at me across the table as if he hadn't heard me right.

I clarified: "I thought the reason people love going to Rincón is because it's semi-deserted."

"Don't be so romantic," he said after a sip of wine. "People like going where people like me tell them they like going. Regardless, that's where you and I'll spend next summer. The resort won't be entirely finished of course, but they've promised to have a couple of the bungalows done in time."

"We've never lived on-site like that before. We've always just stayed here. I've gotten used to it."

"Well, that's part of what I wanted to talk to you about."
He threw a sliver of white cheese into his mouth and chewed
thoughtfully. "Last month we sold the St. Lucia to develop-
ers. Next winter they're going to close it, tear it down, and
start building something new in its place."

My first concern was where the ghost would go.

"You can't destroy the St. Lucia. It's five hundred years
old."

My dad plucked a grape from its stem and shrugged.
"It's out of my hands. For whatever reason the municipal-
ity never added this place to the historical registry, and the
new owners want a building that doesn't require so much
upkeep. You saw the damage Hurricane Irene caused. This
storm could add to it. Buildings come and go," he said with
a laugh. "I think this one's had a pretty good run. Besides, I
thought you'd be more excited about spending more time on
that beach."

That beach. That perfect beach captured by a painting
that hung in Dr. Ford's entryway.

Isabel told me she was sick. Isabel . . .

Marisol is dead.

As if waiting for the most ironically well-timed moment, the lights in the room flickered and faded. The classical music cut out mid-crescendo. My dad cursed under his
breath.

"You want to stay in here?" he asked. "Or ride the storm
out in your room? Either's fine, though I wouldn't mind your

company. And maybe you'd like to talk about what happened last night."

"I'll go back to my room," I replied, silently blessing the outage for giving me good cover for leaving. "I haven't slept very well in the last couple of days." I stood and felt my way through the darkness to the door. When I reached out to the handle I stopped.

"You know that old high-rise hotel on Condado Beach? La Andalusia?"

I heard leather squeak as my dad shifted in his chair. "The abandoned one, yes."

"Why doesn't anyone tear *that* place down?"

"I don't know, Lucas. But I do know that demo for a job that big wouldn't be cheap. Why do you ask?"

"No reason." I opened the door just a crack, but that was enough for the wind to blow it wide. Spray shot into the room, and the plates shook against the table. What must have been my dad's wineglass shattered with a pop against the tile floor. From the far side of the room, I could hear a whoosh as the heavy fabric of the curtains billowed up, followed by the slaps of those curtains beating against the thick glass of the patio doors. Once I'd stepped over the threshold, I dug in my heels, latched onto the doorknob with both my hands, and pulled.

"Stay safe!" my dad yelled over the wind. He rushed up and began pushing the door from the inside. Our combined effort resulted in getting it shut.

Back in my room, I stared at the dark ceiling, and listened

to the storm attack the building. I knocked around the criss-crossing mental images of two tragic girls, one out of myth, the other dead. My forearms still tingled and gave off residual warmth from the rash. Isabel had been right. Isabel, the witch who grants wishes. The blisters had disappeared; the itch was fading. I took out the notes from my pocket. I traced the girls' handwriting, so different from one another's. More than once, I found myself looking at the base of the door, hoping another note would be there.

From Marisol: *It was all a mistake, Lucas. I'm here. Running through the storm. Come find me.*

Or from Isabel: *I'm here, too. Just down the street. Come back.*

I only knew where one girl was, and I went to find her.

On the mezzanine, the porters and housekeepers were shouting in Spanish, asking one another where the stock of candles was so that they could pass them out to all the panicking guests. Here and there a flashlight clicked on. Since I was the last person any of them cared about, no one noticed as I slipped past them and down the stairs.

At the front desk, some of the porters were huddled around a small rabbit-eared television that ran on reserve power, tracking the path of the storm with only mild interest. Others played cards. Clara had finally been the one to find a cardboard box full of votive candles, and I watched as she carried them through the lobby, taking her time and humming a little tune to herself.

I stepped out the front door and stopped. The rain fell diagonally, in swirls and in circles, every way except for down. I couldn't see the street in front of me. The water had risen to the tops of the tires of the cars unfortunate enough to have been left out, and the current was racing toward the sea. A palm frond shot across my field of vision, followed by a twisted mass, maybe a shirt that had been left out on a line. Wind as strong as underwater tides tugged sideways at my clothes. Again, I was completely soaked. Not just soaked: waterlogged. I couldn't even remember the last time I'd felt truly dry.

Hurricanes sound like horror movies. Even when you're outside, it feels like you're shut up in a closet, listening to the wail of sirens and the shrieking sound that wind makes when it's forced through narrow slits. Those sounds would make most people want to hide under their beds and cover their heads to protect their senses while waiting for the chorus of needy spirits to forget about them and move past.

Those sounds do not make most people want to try and run down the middle of Calle Sol, where power lines can spark and snap and land in water, or where heavy limbs can fall from trees and smash in skulls.

The three minutes it would've usually taken to reach Isabel's house dragged out into what felt like an hour. Once

I reached the gate, weather-beaten and with thigh muscles screaming from kicking through two feet of water, I shouted her name and banged on the wood. Wiping my wet hair from my forehead, I tasted bits of salt water carried from the ocean by the wind. Glancing at the courtyard wall, I knew that in this rain and with my legs completely shot, I'd never be able to jump it.

I slammed my fist against the wood again. When there still wasn't any response, I beat against the gate with the heel of my right hand. Splinters tore into wet skin. Rain trailed down my arm and poured from my elbow to the ground.

Finally, the gate flew open. Isabel had me by the front of my shirt. She pulled me through the courtyard and into her house where the rain pelted the glass ceiling above our heads. With her free hand, she slammed the door shut behind us. By the light of several candles throughout the entrance, study, and dining room, I could see that she was wearing the same patchwork pair of jeans from yesterday and a black short-sleeved shirt. Both were soaked.

Isabel's bruise-rimmed eyes flickered across my face. Without her sweatshirt on, she had lost her armor and much of her confidence; she was caught off guard, a poorly prepared antagonist.

"Did anyone see you come in?" she demanded, releasing my shirt and backing away.

"No." I raked my fingers through my wet hair and peered

into the darkened corners of the house. "Is your dad back?"

"No. It's just me."

Isabel took another step back and studied me more intently. I could only imagine what a mess I was: wheezing, soaking wet, anxiously cracking the knuckles of one of my hands, eyes bloodshot from several nights of strange dreams and little rest.

"Listen," I began, catching my breath. "I know I shot out of here yesterday, but I need to know what happened with that wasp."

"You came here during a hurricane so that we could talk about a *wasp*?"

"I want to know what's going on inside this house. You said you were sick. Maybe I can help you."

Isabel tensed; her dark eyes pinched together, and the offer I thought would be met with gratitude was instead met with fury.

"*Help* me?" Isabel asked. "Is that what you just said—that you want to *help* me?"

"Whoa." I put my hands up and took a step back. "I just thought that maybe—"

"Save it. You know what you suffer from, Lucas?" Isabel paused for a moment, searching for the right ammunition. "Hero syndrome. You see every situation as an opportunity for you to come save the day. You think that because I'm sick and there's a storm that I'm here huddled in a corner waiting for Lucas Knight to come knock on my door and ask if he can *help* me? I'm not some imprisoned princess who's desperate for your rescue. I can take care of myself."

I cringed as her words hit their mark. My recent attempts to "save the day" had all failed. My search for Celia had ended before it even began, and my hunt for the phantom Marisol had been in vain. The thing that had sent me over the edge—and straight to Isabel—was knowing that the young nun I'd always hoped haunted my room would never find her love letters and would soon have nowhere to roam. And there was absolutely nothing I could do about any of it.

I wasn't, however, going to give Isabel Ford the satisfaction of knowing how well she had me pegged. I'd found my ammunition, too, and was ready to use it.

"Don't talk like you know me. You were a fiction to me until three days ago, when you started doing everything you could to get my attention. Now that you've gotten what you wanted and I've landed in your house *three* times, you're pissed off about it."

"You coming here has nothing to do with me," Isabel snapped. "It has to do with you wanting to satisfy your burning curiosity."

"You sent the letters! You asked me to come!"

Isabel turned away, dragging her hand through the tangles of her wet hair.

"It was a mistake coming here even once," I said. "It won't happen again."

My hand was already on the door when something massive slammed into the ceiling above me. I ducked, expecting an explosion of glass and debris, but the ceiling held. I peered up, but it was far too dark to see what had fallen.

"Guabancex is mad," Isabel said.

"What?"

"Not *what*. *Who*. Guabancex is the goddess that makes the storms. The Taíno say she gets angry when people upset the balance of her island. She punishes them with storms. She caused the hurricanes that wrecked the Spanish conquistadors' ships. Don't worry, though. The glass will hold."

I swallowed. "Who's upsetting the balance of her island now?"

Isabel shrugged away my question. "Does it matter? You shouldn't go back out there, though. Your skull won't fare as well as this ceiling."

"I'll take my chances," I replied, yanking open the door. The entryway was instantly doused with rain. Isabel dashed forward, slammed the door shut, and bolted it.

"You know I'm right about you," Isabel said, turning to face me. She was just inches away, closer than she'd ever been. I could feel her breath—her breath that kills—hot against the cold wet skin of my neck. It was just one exhale, and then she backed away.

"But you're also right about me," she said more softly. "Just stay. It's dangerous out. I'm sorry I overreacted."

Without giving me the chance to respond, Isabel ducked

through the dining room toward the twisting iron staircase on the other end.

"I'll just be a second," she called out over her shoulder. "I'm going to fetch you a towel and a dry shirt."

My hand was still on the doorknob. It stayed there as the rain and wind continued to buffet the walls of the house. It stayed there as I peered into the study that, aside from being entirely candle-lit, looked almost exactly like the same—in a state of gentlemanly disarray—as it did when I was here last. One thing was different, though. Near the coffee table was a terra-cotta pot holding a thin-stemmed plant about a foot and a half tall. It had delicate green leaves and small purple flowers that resembled orchids, though those leaves and flowers were crisp and half wilted, as if the plant hadn't been watered in several days. I released the doorknob to go over and kneel down near the plant. It gave off that same alcohol reek as the others in the garden.

Isabel was right—my curiosity always got the best of me. I kept barging into her house. I ran after ghosts in the rain even though I knew it made no sense, but sometimes I had no use for sense. I collected insults because I thought the more I had, the closer I would get to invincibility. I was developing a habit of reaching out to touch things—like strange girls and strange-smelling plants with purple petals—that I was sure would hurt me because no matter how severe, the resulting pain was always worth the attempt.

TWELVE

"THAT'S POISONOUS."

I spun around to see Isabel standing in the entrance to the study. She'd changed into a new pair of jeans and an oversized flannel button-up shirt. Her long wet hair hung down loose, shining like fresh tar.

It was there, cast in that particular light, when I noticed that she was not quite beautiful. Everything that I could think to compare her to was bleak. Mostly, it had to do with those eyes of hers: dark on dark. Raven black ringed with deep purple. Hard like bricks. There was no getting past them. I wondered if she wanted anyone to even try.

"This is the largest one I have." She held up a dark gray button-up shirt before gathering it together with a towel and tossing them both to me. Turning around, she cleared her throat. It took me a second to realize she was trying to give me some privacy to change. I stood, stripped off my shirt, pulled on the new one, noticing a tear near the collar that had been expertly mended with red thread. My jeans would just have to stay wet.

"I'm sorry about Celia," Isabel said, which caused my fingers to momentarily freeze on one of the buttons. "I really hope someone's found her."

"How did you know about that?"

"I hear things when I'm in the courtyard. Some of the ladies were talking about it earlier. They said she's Marisol's little sister." Isabel paused. "Did you know her well?"

"Not really. I gave her a charm last night. In the shape of a wolf. I told her to keep it as reminder to be brave. I didn't think it'd make her so brave that she'd go out looking for her sister in the middle of the night on the eve of a hurricane."

"It's not your fault, Lucas. You didn't drive her out into that storm."

"I'm done," I said, rolling up the sleeves of the shirt and desperate to change the subject.

She turned and gestured to the blotches on my arms. "Those look better."

I rubbed my skin absently.

"It's columbine." Isabel pointed to the plant I'd just been hovering over. "Usually they're only found in dry climates, but my dad crossbred a couple of species to get this one that survives in the tropics. I know his personality can be prickly sometimes, but the work he does is remarkable."

"Are there any plants in this place that aren't poisonous?"

Isabel smiled wanly and went over to take a seat at her

dad's cluttered desk. "I'm guessing that's just one of your many burning questions, young Michael Knight."

"And I'm guessing your dad's not the only one around here with a prickly personality."

Isabel put her hand over her heart in mock offense. "I thought we'd called a truce."

"You called it. Not me."

I waited, watching as Isabel looked down to the papers strewn across her dad's desk and started running her fingers—her thin, capable fingers like those of her dad—across them.

"Most of them are poisonous," she said, finally looking up. "Some aren't. Most are."

"Why so many?"

"Because that's what he studies."

"What happened to your mother?"

Isabel frowned—just like I would've. Just like I *did* whenever someone asked me the same question. "That's abrupt."

"They say he loved his plants more than he loved her."

"Is that what *they* say?" The chair Isabel was sitting in squeaked as she leaned forward. "*They* being old señoras with too much time on their hands?"

I never thought I'd be recounting the stories I'd heard about the house at the end of Calle Sol to a person who lived in the house at the end of Calle Sol—it was like telling a ghost story to a ghost—but once the stories started pouring past my lips, they wouldn't stop. I told Isabel about the señoras, how they said her father neglected her mother to the point that she grew so sad she would play her harpsichord while her husband's great bird croaked along, and how Isabel's mother eventually cursed the house, destroyed the bird, then disappeared.

"She wasn't his prisoner," Isabel said.

"The señoras said he loved his macaw and his plants more than he loved her."

Isabel shook her head. "It was a gray. Not a macaw. An African gray. His name was Rios. Papá would teach him to mimic, say things like 'hello' and 'jolly good.' But forget about the bird. What did your friends think about my mother? Did they believe the old ladies?"

"We made up our own stories. Rico said she died in child-birth. Ruben said she jumped off the walls of El Morro."

"And what was *your* story?"

"I didn't want to believe she was dead. I thought maybe she'd stolen a boat and rowed over to St. Croix or Barbados."

Several seconds went by, punctuated by howls from the storm.

Then Isabel said, "I'm sorry to say that none of your stories are true, but, if I had to choose, yours is definitely the best."

"What's the truth, then?"

"Do you really want to know? Do I even have to ask if you really want to know?"

"I think you know the answer to that," I replied.

Isabel was still for a moment. Eventually, she rose from her chair and came to sit cross-legged on the ground in front of the columbine.

"Come sit," she commanded. "And promise you won't run away again."

"I promise. Of course."

"Of course," Isabel softly repeated.

She began to roll the dry purple petals of the columbine between her fingers. The edge of her sleeve slipped back, and in the dim light, I could see a dark bruise on the tender skin between the thumb and index finger of her right hand. It made me think of how, when I was a boy and had a nasty bruise, my mom would rub her thumb over it three times in a circle and then give it a kiss. She told me that made them fade more quickly, and I could have sworn it worked.

"Looks can be deceiving, you know," Isabel mused. "In many ways, these plants seem harmless, but they're good at hiding their true nature. Some have distinctive markings; others you can cut into and tell their toxicity by the color of the sap. With columbine, you're looking for five petals in certain shades of blue or violet, all of which have this particular shape. It's lovely, isn't it?"

My eyes were locked on Isabel's fingers as they stroked those small poison petals, so delicately, with such care.

"I need you to know that after you fell, I *had* to move you." There was a hitch in her voice. She released her hand from the plant, pulled her sleeves over both her fists, and folded her arms across her chest. "It would've been much worse if you'd just stayed where you landed. I covered up my hands the best I could, but sometimes that's not enough."

My eyes were still on the columbine. Its leaves were now green and glistening, its petals revived from their once near-dead state. Isabel did that. I touched my arm, recalling the burning itch, the blurred vision, the delirium and shooting pains. Isabel did that, too.

"It wasn't the plants," I said. "It was you. You made me sick."

Isabel exhaled. "It happens when I touch someone. Or if I'm too close to them for too long. You might be starting to feel sick now—"

"I'm fine," I interrupted.

"You'll probably get sick later then," Isabel said. "But I swear, you falling into all those plants out there made it much worse."

"Plants like these?" I reached out and snapped a leaf from the columbine.

"Lucas!" Isabel unfolded her arms and snatched the leaf from my fingers. "This isn't a game."

"That plant has no effect on you whatsoever?"

Isabel faltered, rolling the leaf between her fingers with such force that it tore and was smashed into fibers and green pulp.

"One of the stories about this house is that there was a baby born here full of poison," I said. "That was you."

Isabel wiped the crushed remainders of the leaf on her jeans. "That was me. The poison builds up. When I'm around my plants, I can transfer some of it to them. If I'm not around them, the poison just keeps building up and up and I get sick. Sicker."

"That's why you stay here."

"That's why I stay here," Isabel echoed. "When I was little, I could go for days without having to be near the plants. I would go with my dad to his labs out near Rincón. You recognized my painting the other day. But now I have to be around the plants almost constantly. I tuck leaves into my sheets when I sleep. I wear them between my skin and clothes, but it doesn't do much good. I don't know what the problem is." She paused. "It's been getting worse since the start of summer."

I asked a question I realized was stupid the second it passed my lips: "Can't your dad do anything?"

"He's trying, Lucas." Isabel collected up her mass of wet hair and whipped it over one shoulder. "Despite your stories, he's not evil. He's just . . . protective. He doesn't want to lose me like he lost my mother."

From the corner of the room, a grandfather clock readied itself to usher in a new hour. I was able to hear the subtle ticks and whirs of gears. I glanced up at the ceiling as the chimes began to toll and saw that individual drops were hitting the glass as opposed to sheet after sheet of water.

I would have to leave soon. I didn't want to.

"What's it called?" I asked, looking back down to Isabel.

She had her eyes fixed on the hem of her jeans, where she'd started to pluck violently at a loose thread.

"What's what called?" she muttered.

"Your illness?"

Isabel smirked. "I'm quite sure it doesn't have a name."

As Isabel continued pulling at the thread, I moved forward, pushing the pot containing the columbine aside, narrowing the space between us. Despite everything I'd seen and heard and experienced over the last two days, I had to sit on my hands to keep them from twitching. They had minds of their own. They didn't want to touch the columbine anymore. They wanted to touch Isabel. The fever that toppled me last night had been transformed by memory into nothing but a minor inconvenience, nothing worse than the outcome of a typical night out drinking.

The questions I'd had, the ones collected over the years about witches and curses, I didn't want to ask anymore of those. New questions had formed—about Isabel. About her life, if you could call it that. About her paintings. About what it was like to hide yourself away and watch and listen. Was it lonely or was it wonderful? Could it be both?

"What would happen if I touched you again?"

Isabel's head snapped up; she again folded her arms across her chest, tighter this time. "Was I unclear about that?"

"Your dad's been around you his whole life—and lived to tell the tale."

"Sometimes by the skin of his teeth. If he had to pick

me up when I fell, he'd get rashes on his hands. If I got sick and he had to be near me for a long time, he'd also get sick—sometimes for days."

"Did you ever think that he might die?"

"Several times." Isabel stood abruptly and bolted past me. A drop of water fell from the tips of her hair onto my hand. "It didn't take much time for him to figure out it's best to stay away from me, and I figured out how to take care of myself. Speaking of that," she continued, flinging open the front door, "you should probably leave. Now that the storm is passing, my dad might be back soon. And, like I said, it's not good for you to be around me very long."

I started to protest, but Isabel had disappeared into the soggy, leaf-strewn courtyard.

Apparently, both of the Fords were terrible at goodbyes.

I stood and, shaking the pins from my legs, followed Isabel into the courtyard. I hopscotched fallen branches, palm fronds, and even a single brown shutter that had been torn from some unfortunate house. It was still lightly raining, but since I was still somewhat damp, it didn't much matter.

The post-storm sky was cantaloupe-colored. In that light, as Isabel undid the latches on the gate, I noticed again her black-rimmed nails and the nasty bruise on her hand, dark purple and yellowed around the edges.

"What happened there?"

Isabel saw where I was looking and shook her head dismissively. "It's nothing. I just bruise easily. Bad blood."

"Can I see it?"

Isabel dropped her hand from the gate and turned to face me. "Why?"

"I just want to see it."

Isabel's mouth twisted into a slight scowl, but she pushed back her sleeve and lifted her hand to where it hovered between us.

"You know," I said, "someone once taught me a way to make bruises like this fade more quickly."

My thumb landed lightly on the center of the bruise, and Isabel's hand immediately tensed. I traced the edges of the bruise three times and moved closer. My lips had barely grazed Isabel's skin before she bit back a scream and hit me across the face.

THIRTEEN

I WAS SICK for three days.

I hadn't even straightened up before Isabel pushed me out
the gate. And after the gate had slammed shut behind me,
and I'd started down Calle Sol with a smile on my face, I
could still hear her calling me bad names in Spanish.

Eventually, I passed the house of Señora Garcia. With
bare feet and a broom clamped in her arthritic fingers, she
was attempting to sweep up the wet leaves and palm fronds
that had fallen in front of her house during the storm. She
was wearing a housedress that came down to her knees, and
her dark varicose veins pulsed across her bare calves as she
worked. She stopped and stared, making sure that I could
see her mumbling at me under her breath.

I waved and gave her my best grin. "Buenos días, Señora."

She spit in the street and went back to sweeping.

I got back to the hotel just in time for my dad to wave me

over for breakfast in the restaurant. The manager apologized for the half-functioning kitchen and delay in fresh coffee. My dad ignored him and continued to read from the soggy, day-old newspaper.

"Did you hear about these girls who went missing?" he asked. "One of them died. Sisters from San Juan, Cara and Marilyn."

"Mari*sol*. Is there something about them in the paper?"

"No." He flipped the page and recrossed his legs. "I heard a couple of the porters talking about them on my way down this morning."

My dad clucked his tongue and said it was a pity that so many young girls in Old San Juan were undereducated and lacked proper guidance. He apparently could not put two and two together to figure out that Mari*sol* was the reason I'd spent close to ten hours at the police station.

"You should really be thankful for what you have, son." He looked up. "Is that a new shirt?"

As I chewed violently on a hunk of banana bread, I envisioned myself swimming out into the ocean, never stopping, never returning.

It wasn't until the first forkful of eggs entered my mouth that I realized my food didn't taste right. I spit the eggs into my napkin, but the courtyard had already started spinning. I had to grip the table to keep from getting dizzy. The skin around my lips started to crawl, like it was being swarmed by tiny beetles. I slapped and scratched to get them off.

I heard my dad call my name. He said I looked terrible and asked if I got enough sleep. I couldn't answer. My tongue felt heavy and numb. As I pushed away from the table, I lost my balance and fell onto one knee. My coffee cup tipped off its saucer and hit the ground, where it smashed into several pieces and sent hot coffee all over my hand. The pain barely registered. The slivers of porcelain turned to worms inching across the wet bricks.

I peeled myself off the ground and managed to stumble up to my room just in time to retch up a mixture of coffee, banana bread, and stomach fluid into the toilet. As I was resting my cheek against the cold porcelain, I realized that Isabel had entirely avoided answering my question about her mother. I smiled, thinking that gave me good reason for another visit. Then I passed out.

I woke up in my bed with one of the housekeepers dabbing my forehead with a damp washcloth. I was burning up. The sheets were soaked. My breaths were thin and made whistling sounds. When I ran my tongue over my dried-out lips, I could feel small blisters around the edges.

I slept and woke, slept and woke, always thirsty. I dreamed. First, of a Christmas back in Houston. I must have been six. I'd gotten a plastic baseball bat and a ball with a stand. Even though it was icy outside, I went into the backyard to play. I imagined a crowd cheering for me as I hit a grand slam and ran the bases, pumping my small fists in the air. I imagined them cheering loud enough to drown out my mother calling my dad a selfish asshole from inside the house.

I dreamed of the dog I was never allowed to have. He was a golden retriever named Frankie. Imaginary Frankie and I went on a long walk around the neighborhood. When we got back home, I filled up his bowl in the backyard and petted his thick hair as he lapped up water.

I dreamed of being with Marisol, kissing her full lips and putting my hands under the thin fabric of her dress in a quiet, empty room. She told me again that she'd waited all year for me to come back to the island. Then she told me she had a secret. In between kisses on my neck and my throat, she told me she was full of poison, and now that she'd kissed me all over, I was full of poison, too. I didn't care. If anything, what she told me made me only want to kiss her more.

I dreamed of my mother; she was standing near a window, with her back to me. She was telling me the story of la ciguapa, the monster who lives in the trees on the edge of the beach. La ciguapa has dark eyes, and her black hair is so long it touches the tops of her feet like the hem of a dress. Her feet are backward so her toes face behind her. She is full of misery and hate. At night, she paces and sings—if you could even call that noise she makes singing. It sounds more like children wailing in an empty church. In the morning, you can trace the path she was walking because of her backward footprints and because rocks and the leaves will be sprinkled with her tears.

La ciguapa is not dead, my mother said in the dream, but she's not alive, either. She roams the trees around the beach looking for the man she once loved a long time ago—some say he was a sailor who went out one morning with his ship and never returned—but as much as she searches, she will never find him.

So she finds substitutes.

I'd heard this story before—not in a dream but for real. My mom had said there was an old man in her village who everyone believed had met the monster. It happened one morning when he went out fishing. La ciguapa was just there, standing at the edge of the tree line, gesturing for him to follow her. He did; he followed her deep into the forest hoping to get a single kiss. She kissed him, yes, but when she pulled away, he realized she'd taken a piece of his spirit. Now when he spoke, he'd trail off in the middle of sentences and leave certain letters out from all his words.

In the dream, I asked my mother if she believed in her, if she thought la ciguapa was real.

My mother smiled. Her answer was perfect: "What's there not to believe?"

Last, I dreamed of the young nun. She sat on the edge of the bed and rubbed my hot feet with her cold hands. She'd been in love with the *blacksmith's* son, not the butcher's son, she told me. She didn't know why everyone kept getting that wrong. Most of the rest of the story was true, though, she'd said with a sigh. My room was once her room. She'd remembered lying right where I was lying, and gazing up at the ceiling, tears running down her cheeks, as the blood drained out of her.

She looked at me. She had no eyes, just fuzzy circles that were as dark as her habit. She told me that some loves are not meant for this world. She asked if I understood; I nodded. I told her they were tearing the hotel down and that I was sorry. I told her I wanted to help her, but she just turned her head and was quiet as she continued to press her dead thumbs into the arches of my feet. Before she left, she walked around the room, looking for her letters one last time. When I told her I'd never seen any as long as I'd been staying here, she seemed disappointed.

Eventually a doctor came, and I was lucid enough to hear her tell my dad I'd contracted some kind of fever. She said it looked like it was breaking, but that it might be causing hallucinations.

No shit, I wanted to say. I've been talking to ghosts.

I slept again for what seemed like days. I dreamed about my mother again, about running through burning buildings, about Marisol, about a little girl who turned into a wolf, about imaginary Frankie, about swimming into the ocean, but never about Isabel.

When I finally woke up, Rico was sitting on the edge of my bed, watching my television. At first I thought I was imagining him, too. I was tired of opening my eyes and feeling like the world had completely changed since the last time I'd shut them. As a test, I closed my eyes slowly and then opened them again, just as slowly. He was still there.

"What are you doing?" I mumbled.

Rico spun around. "Hey! Look who's up! It's La Bella Durmiente!"

"Way to be sick, dipshit." I turned to see Carlos lying beside me, shoeless but still dressed in his porter's uniform. He had something like five pillows under his head. I checked: I had none.

"Make yourself at home," I said.

He grinned. "Don't worry, Lucas. I have been."

"So, what?" Rico asked. "You feel better?"

Surprisingly, I did. I didn't feel like I was burning holes through my sheets while surrounded by figures from my dreams. I put my hand over my heart and confirmed that it was, in fact, still functioning. I licked my lips. The sores were gone—if they'd even been there in the first place.

"One of the ladies who works here said your fever finally broke," Rico said. "So what happened to you, man? Eat something bad? Get bit by a rat?"

"Something like that," I muttered.

I dragged myself out from under the covers and into a pair of jeans that I'd tossed on the floor several days ago. They smelled like piss and old sweat. I'm sure I smelled just as bad.

My legs felt wobbly from lack of use as I made my way to the bathroom, leaving my friends to continue their full-room takeover. After splashing water on my face, I leaned against the sink and looked in the mirror. The skin under my eyes was deep purple; my cheeks and chin were covered with dirty blond stubble, and my hair was so greasy it practically stood on end. What was sad was that I'd seen myself look worse.

"Hey, Lucas!" Carlos shouted from the other room. "The reason we stopped by was to see if you were up to going to the Festival de San Juan tonight."

Every June, the locals all gather in the Plaza de Armas to celebrate San Juan Bautista, the patron saint of the island. Street vendors hock fried codfish, beer, and cheap necklaces made from shells, and little kids run around holding sparklers too close to their faces. Couples old and young dance to live bands consisting of men sharply dressed in their best guayaberas, fedoras, and boat shoes and who can play their instruments all night long. Women come in from the outlying districts in droves in their finest flower-print sundresses and don't leave until the sun comes up or until they find a man, whichever comes first. Kids my age find dark corners where they can drink and feel each other up. Inevitably, either Rico or I—or sometimes the both of us—end up drunk and in the fountain.

"Yeah, sure." I shoved a toothbrush in my mouth. "Hey, so where was Celia?" I asked, stepping from the bathroom. I assumed that she'd found her way home, since she wasn't the first thing either of them brought up.

Rico spoke without turning his head away from the television. "She's still missing, Luke."

I halted mid brush.

"The police are still looking, man," Carlos added. He interlaced his fingers behind his head and snuggled deeper into his mountain of pillows.

I turned to spit in the sink and then dragged the back of my hand across my mouth.

"And you're just okay with that?" I asked, stepping out of the bathroom.

"I know it freaks you out since you and Mari were kind of . . . you know, *close*," Rico added, his eyes still glued on my television, "but we've done all we can do at this point."

"Our friend's cousin vanished into thin air," I said, "and neither of you give a shit."

Rico spun around and launched off the edge of the bed. Before I could dodge him, he'd shoved me hard on both shoulders causing me to crash into the bathroom doorframe. If it had been anyone but Rico, I would've fought back, but Rico's was a rage that hit whiplash-fast. Whenever I lost my temper—which was often enough—no one got legitimately freaked out the way they did when Rico lost his. I'd seen guys react to his anger the way an unfortunate hiker would react to a bear he came across on a trail—hands up, palms out, making soothing sounds while backing away slowly.

"*We* don't give a shit?" Rico snarled. "*We* looked for her. While you were here sick off your ass, Carlos and me were knocking on doors and helping out with search parties, not to mention going to Marisol's funeral and staying up all day and night trying to keep Ruben from completely losing his shit, so don't *fucking* talk to me in that stuck-up way of yours about not caring."

Marisol's funeral. I'd missed it because I was sick. I was sick because I couldn't resist putting my lips on Isabel's skin.

I turned to Carlos, who'd swung his legs off the side of the bed and was in the process of putting his work shoes back on. He looked at me, shook his head, and shrugged like, *What do want me to do?*

"Hey!" Rico shoved me again in the chest to get my attention. "I'm sorry about Marisol, okay? I know you were only together for a couple of days or whatever, but still that sucks." He put his finger in my face, but his tone had softened. "You should've just told me you were going to the beach that night. I would've come with you, and you wouldn't have had to deal with this . . . " He waved his hand in the air. " . . . by yourself."

I cringed. "I wanted to be alone."

"Yes, I know." Rico backed away. "Lucas—always needing his precious alone time. We get it." He ticked up his chin to Carlos. "Let's go."

Carlos was halfway out the door when he stopped and turned. "Hey. I just want you to know—while you were sick La Lopez was around asking questions."

"About what?"

"About you. Like, about your temper. Like, if I've ever seen you get jealous or anything. I told her out of everyone I knew, you were the most levelheaded."

"So you lied?"

"Through my teeth." Carlos cracked a smile that quickly faded. "Just be careful. La Lopez has it out for you."

After they left, I took my time in the shower, scrubbing off the days' worth of grime, then shaved, slicked back my hair, scrounged up some clean clothes, and headed downstairs to have my first proper dinner in a long time. In the staircase, I ran into a girl who had just arrived with her parents after a long flight from the mainland and was out exploring the hotel on her own. She was wearing a long white dress and white leather sandals to match. I told her my name was Luke, that I was from Houston, that my dad owned this place. I wasn't proud of myself, but it just all came out, so easy, like it used to before all the girls I met ended up dead or deadly. The girl smiled. She was pretty. She said her name was Tara and that it was nice to meet me.

"Do you want to take a walk?" I offered. "I can show you some great places around town."

The two of us were halfway through the lobby when I heard my dad call out my name. I could tell by the direction his voice came from that he was in the "library," a rarely used room just off the front entrance that had very little to do with the actual storage and enjoyment of books. It was more like an Old World man-cave, housing clusters of broken-in leather chairs, an antique pool table that no one was allowed to touch, the stuffed and mounted carcasses of various animals in "lifelike" poses, and my dad's personal stock of scotch (which was safely secured in a cabinet to which only he had the key). The only time he ever went in that room was when he was trying to impress someone.

I promised Tara I'd just be a second and headed over to the half-open set of twelve-foot-high, seventeenth-century wooden doors. When I entered the room, I saw that my dad wasn't alone. There, settled across from him at one end of an overstuffed brown leather couch and holding a snifter of brandy, was Dr. Rupert Ford.

The color in both his and my dad's cheeks indicated that they'd been in high spirits for a while. Sitting there, both impeccably dressed and getting sloshed on a bottle of liquor that probably cost more than three of Carlos's paychecks combined, the two of them looked like old friends. For all I knew, they were.

"Son!" My dad set his glass down and leaned forward as I stepped into the room. "How are you doing? Have you heard anything about your friend's cousin? Clara, was it?"

"Celia," I replied, trying not to stare at the doctor's long fingers curling around the short stem of his snifter as he swirled the amber-colored liquid. "And, no."

"Your father's told me what you've been going through the last few days." Dr. Ford lifted the thin glass up to his mouth and took a sip, wincing from the alcohol burn. "Loss. Grief. Sickness. So unfortunate."

The silence that followed stretched to an uncomfortable length.

"So, Lucas," my dad eventually said. "Rupert came over to tell me that you paid him a visit recently."

Shit.

"Apparently you're interested in studying botany." He looked over at Dr. Ford and chuckled. "That's news to me."

I cracked a knuckle as I tried to come up with a decent response.

"Yeah, well when you asked about college visits the other day, it got me thinking," I said. "Since I like it so much out here, I thought it might make sense for me to stay for college."

My dad's eyes shimmered, I hoped from the booze and not from some newfound fatherly pride. In a way, I was disappointed he couldn't see through my flimsy attempt at deception.

I went on. "Science seemed like a good idea. You know, because of all the nature."

All the nature. What a dumb thing to say.

Dr. Ford thought so, too. He again brought the snifter up to his lips, though now he was visibly sneering.

"I think that's great, Lucas!" My dad picked up a large leather-bound book from one of the side tables and held it out to me. "You couldn't have picked a better mentor. I asked Rupert to bring over one of his manuscripts so that we could add it to our library. I also took the liberty of having him inscribe it for you."

Once the book was in my hands, I turned to the blue cursive on the title page. The handwriting was similar to, but not quite the same as, Isabel's.

To the young Michael Knight. Best of luck with your scientific endeavors. Warmest regards, Rupert Ford III.

"It's apparently groundbreaking stuff," my dad added.

Dr. Ford shook his head and put up his hand in a show of false modesty. "It's a minor text. I wrote it when I was a young man not much older than Lucas here. It's about Puerto Rico, naturally, and all the species of poisonous plants that grow on the island. They're my specialty, as you know. And while it may not be as exciting as the things most young people read today, it's still relevant to your burgeoning interest."

"Thanks," I said, itching to get away. My dad and Dr. Ford together, acting all buddy-buddy—it was not something I wanted to see. "Can you just leave it here?" I handed the book back to my dad. "I'll come back and look at it later."

"Sure, Luke. You on your way out? Rupert and I were just about to head over to the restaurant and have dinner. We wouldn't mind if you joined us."

I tried not to smirk as I thought about just how much Rupert Ford would mind if I joined them for dinner.

"I'm good. Hey, I heard Mara Lopez has been around here asking questions about me."

My dad grunted. "That foul woman. Some people here just have it out for people like us."

"It's true." Dr. Ford nodded. "Distrust is embedded into their culture—particularly distrust of foreigners of a certain means." He turned toward me and held up his snifter. "Take care, then, Mr. Knight."

I took that as my cue to leave.

As I closed the door behind me, I heard, in addition to the clinking of glasses, my dad asking the doctor if he cared for another nip.

I needed Tara to forget, and to regress. So, as promised, I took her around to the best of the old Spanish-style buildings and snapped a picture of her in front of the statue of Ponce de León. After that, I led her down to the footpaths outside of El Morro and showed her the old mangrove trees.

It was all going well enough until I made one major mistake. We were walking along the waterfront when I asked Tara if she'd ever thought about jumping into the ocean water and swimming until she sank. Once the words left my mouth, she stopped and stared at me like I was demented, and as I studied her face by the blood-orange light of the setting sun, I tried not to picture her hair, wet and tangled in my toes, or her dead eyes fixed on the moon. It was impossible.

I wasn't surprised when our date ended there, even though my original plan was to lead her back to my room in the hopes of drinking stolen wine until our thoughts and lips and fingertips grew numb and we fell into each other's arms.

Instead, I went back to my room alone and lay awake for hours, trying and failing to fall asleep. This made sense, given that I'd been unconscious for three whole days.

Eventually, I went downstairs and paused in front of the library, picturing the expensive scotch behind its doors. Maybe my dad had left his liquor cabinet unlocked.

No such luck. I stayed in there anyway, taking a seat in one of the plush leather chairs and staring at all the books I'd never read. Dr. Ford's was still out on one of the side tables. I snatched it up and flipped to the title page. Above his signature was an incomprehensible title about tropical flora. If I couldn't understand the title, there was little hope in me getting through the rest.

On the next page was the dedication: *To Zabana. There is nothing in this or any world strong enough to divide us.*

Zabana. The woman who must have given Isabel her dark features. I skimmed past the table of contents to the first lines of the first chapter:

Hot as a hare, blind as a bat, dry as a bone, red as a beet, and mad as a hatter. Doctors memorize this phrase to aid them in identifying the symptoms of poisoning. It is true that many of the solandra *species of poisonous tropical plants native to* the island of Puerto Rico, such as cup of gold, have long been used for ceremonial and hallucinogenic purposes. There are descriptions in the diaries of the Spanish settlers of the Taíno ingesting cup of gold during their religious ceremonies. The natives would report developing fevers, having blurred vision, desperately needing water, and undergoing vivid, psychotropic experiences.

"Tell me about it," I mumbled.

These sensations, however, have little to do with any kind of spiritual experience. They are merely the result of changes in brain and body chemistry brought about by poison.

The chapter continued, but I stopped and turned to the index. The specific plant that I was looking for was discussed on page forty-eight.

Legend dictates that lions eat the flowers of the columbine during the spring mating period to give themselves extra vigor. Therefore, some people have taken to rubbing the petals of the columbine against their bare skin when they are in need of a touch more courage.

Columbine has also become a popular symbol for in-gratitude or forsaken love, and thus it is fitting that Ophelia mentions the flower (among many others, of course) in Shakespeare's Hamlet.

As intriguing as these stories may be, they are just that: stories. They are invented and passed on to mask the realities of poisonous plants and their effects on humans, for it is not

remarkable if one merely is sick; he or she must be lovesick.
Nor is it enough that a man have innate courage; he must have
obtained it from some magical source.

I shut the book and carried it upstairs, but when I tossed it on my bed, it fell open to a page near the middle that had been marked with what on first glance appeared to be a roughly two-inch-wide green-and-yellow bookmark. It didn't take me long to realize, however, that it wasn't a bookmark, but a smashed segment of a leaf from the dumb cane plant that I'd seen sitting near the Fords' doorstep. The fact that its colors were still fresh and vivid and it gave off an acrid scent told me it had been recently torn from its stem.

Was this some kind of a threat? Had Dr. Ford found out about my recent tumbles into his house and was letting me know—*again*—to stay away from things that were, as he'd put it, a "bit of an irritant"?

Like I cared.

I used one of the pillowcases to take the leaf from the book and place it on my nightstand. Then, finally surrendering to the reality that this would be a sleepless night, I headed out into the drizzle. I'd eventually head to Festival de San Juan. But first, I had to stop and see a saint.

FOURTEEN

AFTER SAINT PIUS died in Rome during the second century, his hair and nails grew to great lengths and his corpse was sealed in wax. Then for whatever reason, Saint Pius's mummified, wax-covered corpse took a trip across the Atlantic Ocean and ended up in a glass casket in middle of the San Juan Cathedral.

There are lots of saints there; their freaky wood and plaster likenesses watch over the space and care for the prayers that live as long as the little red candles stayed lit.

But Saint Pius isn't made of wood or plaster. His weird, shrunken body is actually there—along with his ghost, if the stories are true. His leatherlike skin and brittle bones are perfectly preserved, along with the light brown hair that falls over his shoulders. When I was a kid, I would tiptoe up to his glass coffin and stare, waiting for his fingers to twitch. They never did. His permanent immobility gave me the creeps way more than if he were to suddenly sit up and turn his head to look at me.

I'd lit three of those little red candles—one for Sara, one for Marisol, and one for Celia—and had taken a seat in one of the pews within view of the saint—just an eyelid twitch would do—when I heard the clicking of footsteps coming down the aisle. Whoever it was scooted down the row directly behind mine, and sat down. The wood squealed. A Bible was lifted out of the compartment on the back of my pew. I could hear its pages swish as they were flipped.

Then, there was my name, spoken in a raspy whisper: "Lucas."

I turned and came face to face with Detective Mara Lopez. As always, her black hair was pulled away from her face and slicked down.

"You remember me, don't you?" She smiled with her thin, red-stained lips and then opened the flap of her dark trench coat in order to flash her badge. "From last summer? We spoke again the night you found Marisol Reyes, though I don't blame you if you don't remember that last encounter. You were pretty shaken up."

Shaken up. That was putting it mildly.

"I remember." I tried to keep my voice low but was still on the receiving end of a sharp look from an old lady kneeling in one of the pews in front of me.

The detective leaned forward and rested one of her hands

on my shoulder. The crimson color on her fingernails almost exactly matched her lips.

"What are you doing here?" She nodded in the direction of the prayer candles. "Paying your respects?"

"I missed Marisol's funeral."

"Yes, I noticed that."

Something hung between us in the silence that followed, like static in the otherwise stale church air. Why would she notice that I missed Marisol's funeral? Why would she care?

"Is there something I can help you with?" I shifted in my seat. "I have to be somewhere in a little while."

"Ah, yes." She clucked her tongue and nodded. "The festival, right?"

With her hand still on my shoulder, she leaned in closer as if to tell me a secret. Her clothes gave off the slightly sour smell of cheap fabric having been worn too long and too often.

"I just need a moment . . . " She held up her other hand and pinched the air with her pointer finger and thumb, ". . . un momento—of your time. We can just walk down to the plaza together, if you don't mind?" Her eyes darted over to a flower-draped statue of Saint Mary. "This place has too many sets of ears, if you know what I mean."

She stood and began to make her way down the pew and toward the aisle. I let out a long, loud exhale and followed.

It was only after we were both outside and walking through the drizzle on near-empty streets that I asked how she knew where to find me.

"I usually find the people I'm looking for in one of two places: in church or at a bar. And apparently you don't have a cell phone."

"I do back in Houston." I crossed my arms over my chest. "But I never bring it to the island. What it is you wanted to talk to me about?"

"Marisol Reyes."

"Okay. But I don't know what I could say that I haven't already said before."

Sighing, she stuffed her hands in the pockets of her coat. "I knew you'd say that, and I know this must be difficult for you. So, here it is. As you probably know, the official story is that Marisol drowned. Aside from being washed up the way she was, the autopsy report came back saying that there was a large amount of water in her lungs."

The detective paused, giving me the chance for that to sink in. From where we were, the music from the festival was rising into the night sky. I could hear the sharp, low pops of drums.

"And?"

"And . . ." She looked down at the cobblestones and furrowed her brow. "I'm not so sure about that. At the station, you said something about her neck and face being covered in sores."

I stopped and turned to face the detective. She was short, shorter than I remembered, but in that moment she commanded space like someone twice her size. Her jaw was clamped tight as if her mother taught her that if she couldn't say anything nice, she shouldn't say anything at all.

"I said *what?*"

Detective Lopez reached into her coat, pulled out a small pad of paper, and flipped through its pages.

"Yeah. Here it is." She tapped a red nail against the pad. "When asked to describe the condition of her body, you said, and I quote, 'I could only see parts of her—like her neck, throat, and face and fingertips, but they had sores on them, like the kind you'd get from rubbing up against poison ivy or something.'" She glanced up, cocking her eyebrow. "You don't remember saying that?"

I resisted the urge to scratch at my own skin. "No. I was kind of disoriented that night."

"Believe me, Lucas, I understand," she said. "And normally, this wouldn't be a big deal. I mean, bodies in the ocean come in contact with all manner of natural and unnatural objects, and when they wash up they're typically bloated and nearly unrecognizable."

In the attempt to erase yet another sudden, unsettling vision of a dead Marisol, I slammed my eyes shut and pressed my palms into my eyelids. We were now just a block away from the festival. The drums were louder; their sound bounced against the sides of my skull.

"Why are you telling me this?" I asked.

"Yes." I opened my eyes and swiveled my head around to

see the detective stabbing the air with her pointer finger. "Good question."

Together, we rounded the corner and entered the Plaza de Armas. It was exploding with life—a far cry from the hushed and nearly vacant church we'd recently left. There had to have been hundreds of people there, all shouting and laughing over the sounds of clinking beer bottles and drumbeats. Rows of white string lights hung overhead. Pink and purple paper lanterns tilted in the breeze. Over by the fountain, near where I thought I'd seen Marisol on the night of the hurricane, four women were dancing a bomba to the beat of the drums. They clutched the folds of their long, full banana-yellow skirts, exposing their expanse of fabric. They stomped and twirled and arched their backs the way bullfighters do when they strut for the crowd and taunt their bulls.

A little girl about Celia's age ran in front of us. She held a red ribbon high above her head. It fluttered in the air like her own personal comet.

Detective Lopez leaned in so I could hear her over the crowd noise. "I wanted you to know that, as far as I'm concerned, Marisol's case is still open. Same goes for Sara Fikes. Both of the girls were found in the same general area, and they were in a similar physical condition. What you said that night—about their bodies—got me thinking these cases might be more than your standard-issue drownings."

Mara Lopez paused again, this time to size me up with her clever, searching eyes. I knew she was gauging my reaction, studying the ways my facial muscles twitched, taking mental notes. It was obvious she'd not just found me out to relay information. She wanted something from me; she thought I was guilty of something; she'd always thought I was guilty of something. In her eyes, she was a hammer, and I was that one stubborn nail that would never slam into place.

"I never said anything about *their* bodies. I only saw Marisol's. You said on the news that her condition was consistent with that of a drowning victim."

"I did say that, didn't I?"

"So what happened?" I demanded.

"I'm still working on figuring that out, but in the meantime, if there's anything you can remember—anything that pops into your head—that Marisol might have said or done that could help me out, be sure to let me know."

My response was flat, short: "I've already told you everything I know."

She cocked her head, sharp like a marionette. "Well, you may think that, but there's this thing called repression. We see it a lot with witnesses. It's like you forget certain ... *details* about an event, especially if those details are desagradable."

"I know what repression is."

"Is that right?"

Yeah, that was right. And I hadn't forgotten any of the details about that night, particularly the desagradable ones. I couldn't forget them if I tried.

She reached into her coat again, this time to produce a

business card. Several seconds passed before I took it and shoved it in my back pocket.

"Just think about it," she added. "You'd be surprised how even the smallest detail can crack a case."

Just as she said *crack* the crowd erupted into applause: The bomba had ended. The dancers in front of the fountain stood frozen in triumph.

"Is that it?" I shouted over the applause. "People are waiting for me."

"Your friends? I spoke with a couple of them. Ruben Reyes said you have a temper. That you broke down his door."

What the hell, Ruben?

At this point I had choices: I could act meek, apologetic, shake my head regretfully and say that she and I got off on the wrong foot, that I wasn't the insufferable snob she thought I was, that when it came to me and my dad, the apple fell far, far from the tree. Or, I could tell her to back the hell off, that I just went through a trauma and wasn't going to play the part of the villain in whatever bullshit narrative she was constructing. Or, I could choke down my pride, force a smile, say thanks, tell her I would call if and when any deep, dark memories resurfaced and then wait for Mari and Sara's cases to close so I could get on with my life.

"Is everything all right, Lucas?"

"Fine," I said, looking La Lopez in the eyes and matching her patronizing grin with one of my own. "I'll be sure to let you know if I remember anything."

I should've just stayed home. Even at one in the morning and with the light rain, the plaza was packed; bodies were crammed up against each other and into every conceivable space. Normally, I would've loved that, the wild crush of humanity, but that night it felt like I was drowning.

After Detective Lopez left me, I milled around the edges of the crowd for a while. Just before the band kicked into a new song, I turned at the sound of a shrill whistle. It was Rico. He was waving his right arm over his head to try and get my attention from across the plaza.

I sized up the number of bodies between myself and Rico and sighed. As I pushed through, the crowd seemed to give off a collective rumble. Fingers hooked my clothes. Arms and legs in mid-twirl flew out in front of me, whacking against my shoulders and my shins. The mingled, cloying scents of cheap cologne, sweat, and spilled beer flooded my nose.

A woman laughed, high and loud, to my right, causing my head to snap in that direction. There, through the tangle of arms and legs and long skirts, I thought I saw a dark figure in a narrow alley between two buildings. I stopped and squinted.

It was Dr. Ford. He was crouched down in front of the little girl I'd seen earlier, the one with the red ribbon. But now, instead of being displayed proudly in the air, the ribbon was hanging limply down by her side. Dr. Ford, dressed just as he had been earlier in the library, in his brown herringbone suit and dark wide-brimmed hat, was talking to the girl. She was smiling as if she knew him.

"Lucas!"

I spun around to see Rico. Next to him was Carlos. They both had bottles of beer. Rico's looked fuller, so I grabbed it from him and took a long pull.

"Let's get out of here!" Rico hollered as he paddled his arms through the air, in a motion I took to mean that he wanted to head to the beach. "This sucks! Too many people!"

He'd read my mind. The heat coming off the crowd was making me feel as if my fever was flaring back up, and I craved the shock of jumping into a cold ocean.

Rico turned and began digging through the crowd. Carlos gave me a shove, my cue to lead the way through the masses.

"Lucas! Lucas Knight!"

I stopped short at the sound of Rupert Ford's unmistakable voice, which caused Carlos to slam into me from behind and spill his beer all over my shirt.

"Damn, Luke! Watch it."

"Go with Rico," I shouted, after turning to see Dr. Ford cutting through the crowd. "I'll find you guys at the edge of the plaza. Don't leave without me."

Carlos shrugged before going on.

As Dr. Ford got closer, I noticed the flush in his face and the moisture that rimmed his red eyes. He was still drunk. But beyond that, he was furious—his jaw was clenched, the skin there pulled tight. The cords of his neck bulged.

He stopped in front of me, not bothering to hide his derision as he looked me up and down. "Is that a new shirt?"

An unexpected tremor rattled up my spine. I didn't even have to look to know that I was wearing the shirt Isabel had let me borrow the night of the hurricane. Housekeeping must have taken it and washed it and put it with all my other clothes while I was sick. I reached up and felt around the collar, and sure enough there was the mend.

"You are such a fool," Dr. Ford hissed. "The more you come around, the more attention you draw, and the more suspicious people get. You realize that if these people find out about her," he said, his eyes scanning the crowd, "they will draw certain conclusions. They will take either her or me away, and she will die. Is that what you want?"

"I wasn't planning on . . . " I stammered.

Dr. Ford cut me off as he leaned in closer and gripped my shoulder with his strong, lean fingers. I glanced at his wrist and thought I saw a rash there on his skin, just underneath his rolled-up sleeve.

"As dangerous as you know Isabel to be, she is not intentionally so." His breath was heavy with the smoky scent of scotch. "She truly hates the fact she has the capacity to bring suffering to others. I, on the other hand, could not care less. And because of that, I will cause you even greater pain than you have already recently suffered if you do *anything* that could lead to my daughter and me becoming separated."

Dr. Ford could've threatened me all day, and it wouldn't have made a difference. Thinking about what might happen to Isabel if people found out she existed, however, was enough to make me quake with fear.

What had Ruben said when I'd gone over to his house after Marisol had died: that nobody wanted me around, that my being there made everything worse?

Is that what I did to every situation I found myself in—made it worse?

"I'm not going to tell anyone about her," I said.

"I saw you speaking to the detective." Dr. Ford's fingers dug into my shoulder. "Just now."

"That had nothing to do with Isabel. That woman hates me. You heard my dad. If she could pin every crime that happens in San Juan on me, she would."

"Maybe for good reason," he shot back. "You certainly have a history of stirring up trouble and not considering the consequences of your actions."

"I'm not a criminal."

"Not yet." Dr. Ford searched my eyes for a moment. His expression was like the detective's: knife-wielding, crafty, hunting for ways to make means justify an end. He finally released my shoulder and gestured to the far end of the plaza. "I believe your friends are waiting for you."

I said nothing, but stared for a moment at Dr. Ford's bloodshot eyes and the lines that spidered from their corners. There was nothing I could say. An apology would've rung hollow with him—a promise would've done the same.

Like the detective, he hated me and would always hate me for breaking into his world.

Someone—a stranger, an obliviously happy festival-goer—bumped into my shoulder, and broke my standoff with Dr. Ford. He stayed put as I turned and began to snake my way through the crowd to where Carlos and Rico were waiting with an idling taxi. They were yelling at me to get a move on. Behind me, in the plaza, the band ended another song, and another cheer rose up.

"Who was that?" Carlos asked, climbing into the cab.

"No one. A friend of my dad's."

Carlos let it drop; for him, it was a good enough explanation.

On the way to the beach, as Carlos and Rico sang along to the cab's radio at the top of their lungs, I was preoccupied by thoughts about Dr. Ford's arms, blotched and inflamed, with tiny white blisters dusting his skin like rock salt. I'd seen those blisters on my own skin after I'd fallen into Isabel's courtyard. They'd come along with a burning fever and delirium, slurred speech and bloodshot eyes. When I'd gone back to the hotel and looked at myself in the mirror, I'd looked . . . *deranged*. Tonight, Dr. Ford had looked the same.

Isabel could do that to a person—mar them inside and out, tip and tilt them from their core. She could, of course, also do much worse.

FIFTEEN

I'D MISSED THE ocean—I hadn't realized how much. I stripped off my shirt and my jeans, tossed them in the sand, and sprinted toward the surf in my boxers. The water, I noticed as I plunged into it, seemed off: strangely cold, with a slightly fungal scent and a less salty taste on the tongue. The recent storms must have brought new water in from far away.

Rico and Carlos were shouting nearby. When I looked over, I could barely make out their heads bobbing up and down and their arms flailing as they tried to dunk each other. I stayed where I was, floating on my back and letting the cold water soothe the memory of my once-burning skin. The seaweed that the storms had uprooted grazed against my legs and my back. I imagined they were the fingers of dead men.

Eventually the three of us raced through the water, parallel to the coastline. It was a dirty fight, and one that I would have won had Rico not whacked me in the face with his fist.

I saw stars, swallowed a mouthful of black salt water, and thought for moment that my nose had been broken.

Almost thirty minutes later, we were laughing, bone-tired, as we pulled ourselves out of the ocean and back onto the beach where we swatted at stray mosquitoes and stumbled around to find our clothes. Carlos tripped over a beach chair and fell face down in the sand. When he tried to get up, he tripped and fell again. The more he told us to shut up, the harder we laughed.

When I finally got back to my room at the hotel, it was nearly dawn. I cracked open Dr. Ford's book in bed, but it almost immediately slipped from my hands and landed on my chest as I fell asleep.

In the morning, I woke feeling a pinch on my face. I slapped my cheek, but the mosquito was quick. He flew over to the nightstand, where he landed on the dumb cane leaf. He took a few light steps, exploring with his slender proboscis. Then he froze. His legs actually seemed to crack in half before he tipped over dead.

Outside my door, I heard the sounds of mild chaos, mostly the hustle of feet, commands given in harsh whispers, and the squeals of carts being pushed swiftly across the mezzanine.

Another mosquito landed on my arm. This one was slower, already fat. I was able to smash it against my skin, where it left a bloody streak.

On my nightstand, my phone rang. It was my dad, telling

me that breakfast in the courtyard was cancelled. He asked me to join him in his room, where he had already rung for room service.

"The mosquitoes are back," he said before he hung up.

Every few years, from the islands to the east, millions of mosquitoes make a giant journey for their tiny bodies. Like ships, they follow the winds and the tides. Once they reach San Juan, they bounce from one thing with blood to another, attacking stray dogs as they run yelping for shelter under cars and zooming down gutters and sewers for lizards and rats. They cause the cats to howl and seek shelter up trees. They squeeze their way through the nets and screens designed to keep them out, burrow down into the folds of blankets, and find warm skin.

A few years ago, hundreds of Puerto Ricans died of the dengue plague. The mosquitoes infected people with poison that caused their faces to swell to the point where their eyes were visible only as slits. People bled from their mouths and noses; their very own blood turned to venom.

Back then, everyone stayed indoors and went crazy. The authorities came on the news and told us the solution was to get rid of standing water. I'd laughed. It's like they didn't even know the composition of their own island.

I had a different solution. I rubbed my arms, legs, and neck with cedar and eucalyptus oil—a trick I'd gained from the wise señoras—before throwing on jeans and a plaid button-up over my white T-shirt. I was almost to the door when I stopped and spun around. With my hands wrapped in toilet paper, I tore up the dumb cane leaf and flushed it down the toilet so that the housekeepers wouldn't accidentally touch it if and when they came into my room that day.

Out on the mezzanine, the brief chaos had settled. It was quiet. There were only the faintest human sounds behind sealed doors. I squinted into the bright morning sunlight, and everywhere were tiny black bodies hovering, leaping over and across one another, diving like kamikazes.

My dad's door was seven down from mine and around a corner. He must have heard my shoes hitting the tile as I ran in his direction, because he opened the door just as I reached it.

"It's bad," he said, simultaneously fastening the latch behind us and slapping a mosquito off his wrist. "They're saying it might be worse than last time."

I collapsed into a chair and poured myself coffee from a French press. On the other side of the room, facing me, the television was muted but tuned to the local morning news show.

My dad took a seat across from me and raked a hand through his hair. "I hate being stuck here."

He raised his coffee cup to his lips, and I couldn't help but notice how different he looked. Unlike himself. His hair was dirty and separated into clumps from yesterday morning's application of pomade. He may have been wearing the same pants and shirt from the suit I saw him in last night in the library.

I dipped my head to hide a sly grin as the question formed on my lips: *Rough night?*

Instead, I asked, "So, how did your dinner go?"

"Oh, fine." My dad sighed as he rubbed his right temple in the attempt to massage away a hangover. I'd been there.

He picked up a piece of toast and started spreading mango butter on it. A mosquito landed near his left collarbone. It crept around some and then stopped. My dad failed to notice. I leaned over and slapped it away.

"I saw Dr. Ford in the plaza last night," I said. "At the Festival de San Juan."

My dad took a bite of his toast and then chewed it with a look of consternation.

"Huh. He told me after dinner that he was heading home. Perhaps he got detoured. Did you get a chance to speak to him?"

I didn't answer. As I brought my coffee cup to my lips, my eyes landed on the muted television. In the corner of the screen, next to the newscaster's head, were school pictures of Marisol and Celia. Mari appeared slightly younger but was smiling broadly in the same way I'd seen her smile the night she attempted to leap into the house at the end of Calle Sol. She'd been beautiful before the ocean I loved so much took her beauty away and covered her with . . . *sores*, as Mara Lopez had said: small, ripped, and white, the type you'd get from rubbing against poison ivy or . . .

Oh God.

I attempted another sip of coffee, but my hand was shaking so badly, the coffee sloshed over the rim. With barely functioning fingers, I set the cup down heavily. Porcelain dishware clattered across the tabletop.

My dad launched out of his chair, and in an uncharacteristically considerate gesture, placed his palm across my forehead.

"Lucas, what's the matter? You're not sick again, are you? Did you check this morning for bites?"

"Yes." I shook my head frantically. "I mean, no. I'm fine."

He backed away to examine my eyes. "Were you drinking last night?"

"No! I . . . Not really, I . . . " I stuttered, searching for an excuse. "I just remembered I told Ruben's mom that I'd go over and keep the family company today. I'm kind of dreading it, that's all."

My dad put his hand on my shoulder and gave it a squeeze. I looked to his face and saw that his expression had softened.

"It's a rough time, I know, but it's good of you to go over there. Just try to be indoors as much as possible today, all right?"

He did know what it was like to have someone disappear on him. The anxiety. The loneliness. I always forgot that.

Mara Lopez was about to start another press conference. I stood, grabbed the remote from my dad's nightstand, and unmuted the television.

". . . mentioned previously, the girls' condition was fairly consistent with that of drowning victims, but we still have to run toxicology tests. The initial results have come back inconclusive, and a second round of testing is currently underway. On behalf of the San Juan Police Department, I'd like to apologize to the families of Sara Fikes and Marisol Reyes and assure them that we are working expediently to bring them closure. When we have conclusive results from the coroner's office, we'll be able to share with the families what exactly caused their daughters' deaths, drowning or otherwise."

Lopez paused to take a question from a man off camera.

"Missing persons is responsible for the case of Celia Reyes," she responded, leaning into the microphone, "so they would be the ones best able to answer that question. Right now we do not believe that the Reyes sisters' cases are linked, but that this is more likely a very, very tragic coincidence."

"Lucas," I heard my dad say from behind me, "maybe you shouldn't watch this if it's too upsetting for you."

"All I can say definitively, as of this very moment—and I want to emphasize how early we are in these investigations— is that, upon further inspection, it now appears as if both of the young women were afflicted with some kind of rash that's inconsistent with what we typically see of drowning victims and more consistent with an allergic reaction. Their legs and arms were covered in red rashes and small white blisters. We're hoping to nail down what might have caused that condition with the next round of testing, but this is going to conclude our remarks for right now."

I heard my dad again ask if I was feeling alright and urge me to have a sit and drink some water. I shrugged him off and charged out the door, across the mezzanine thick with mosquitoes, past my room, down the stairs, through the courtyard, through the lobby, and out the front door.

Then I ran.

Calle Sol was deserted but alive. The normally clear blue sky was speckled with swaying black dots. Those black dots gave off a persistent, angry hum.

Dr. Ford had warned me in no uncertain terms not to come back to his house, but that wasn't a warning I was going to heed. I knew of only two things that could cause reactions like the ones Detective Lopez had just described: Isabel's plants and Isabel.

SIXTEEN

WHEN THE HOUSE at the end of Calle Sol came into view, so did the small-framed figure of a girl sliding through its wooden gate. A hood-covered head snapped in my direction for a split-second before the figure disappeared into the courtyard. I broke into a sprint and then skidded to a stop in time to hear the gate's system of latches snap into place.

"Isabel!" I yelled. "Let me in!"

The metal continued to click. Mosquitoes hummed around my head. Underneath that mix of sounds, I could hear Isabel's labored breaths, wheeze-like, on the other side of the door.

"You don't understand!" Her voice was shrill, on the edge of desperation. "Please, Lucas. Just leave us alone!"

It was the wrong thing for her to demand. I backed away from the gate and crossed the street. With the help of a running start, I catapulted myself up and over the courtyard wall, and landed solidly on my feet, my right arm barely brushing against the leaves of the nearest tangle of plants.

Isabel was running to the door of the main house. I lunged toward her and grabbed her by the sleeve of her sweatshirt. I spun her around to face me, and instantly wished I hadn't.

The last few days had robbed Isabel of all color. Her chapped, ash-gray lips were set in a grimace. Pencil-thick streaks of white ripped through her dark hair. The flesh around her cheeks and jaws stuck more closely to the bone. Her eyes, still raven-black, were huge, slick, and shimmering. Those eyes were once one of Isabel's impenetrable defenses—hard like bricks. Not anymore. Not now. Now they were fathomless—twin pools of guilt and resignation.

"Isabel," I croaked, "what did you do?"

"I...I didn't..." She lowered her head so that most of her face was obscured by her hood. "I'm sorry."

Until then, I'd never believed someone's heart could actually sink, but that's what mine did. It loosened a little, grew sore and heavy, and then dropped.

"My daughter claims you have some sense, Mr. Knight, though I've yet to see you exercise it."

Dr. Ford stood in his doorway. He, like my dad, had not fully come together after the night before. He was dressed again in a brown suit, though his jacket was off, and the top two buttons of his shirt were undone. Locks of graying hair fell across his forehead and formed tight curls.

My fingers went slack, and Isabel tore herself away from me.

"That's better," Dr. Ford said, stepping back from the threshold and gesturing to his entryway.

I glanced over at Isabel. Her body was tense and trembling; she was a girl set to boil.

"Your daughter is wrong," I said, once again entering the house at the end of Calle Sol. I had no sense. It occurred to me I might end up dead and washed up on the beach, but I didn't care. I followed Dr. Ford as he veered left into the dining room; Isabel trailed a few steps behind, her hands buried in the depths of the front pocket of her sweatshirt.

Dr. Ford took a seat and drummed the pads of his fingers against the top of the dining room table. The sound it made was like rain on a rooftop.

"I'm assuming you're here because you saw something on the news this morning that confused you," he said. "From what your father tells me, you're an impetuous and also quite impressionable young man who makes poor choices and fails to listen to reason." He glanced over at his daughter and then back to me. "Just because a couple of girls have an allergic reaction doesn't mean . . . "

Isabel cut off her father by slamming her fist down on the table. Both Dr. Ford and I watched the small object she'd been holding in her hand skitter and spin across the wood. Within seconds, it stopped, and that's when I recognized the head of a wolf, rough hewn from pewter.

"Enough," Isabel growled. "Where is the girl?"

"You know I don't know," Dr. Ford scoffed.

"I said *enough!*" Isabel's voice rose into a near-feral screech. "Where is Celia? Is she dead like the others?"

Dr. Ford's gaze was directed at the table, not to the pewter charm that lay inches from his face, but to the swirling wood grain he was tracing with his pointer finger.

"It was you?" I whispered. "What did you do to them?"

Dr. Ford didn't look up. Instead, he made a sound, an exhale, like a huff, as if this entire conversation wasn't worth his time.

It was then that everything snapped together: Isabel was sick and getting sicker. She'd told me her dad was trying to help her. Mara Lopez was right. Marisol and Sara didn't drown. And even though Isabel could've killed them, she didn't. The girls were dumped in the ocean after having been taken and poisoned and studied by someone whose life revolved around toxic plants and their effects on the human body.

"You experimented on them?"

I started toward the doctor, and he jumped to his feet. But before I could reach him, Isabel launched herself across the top of the table and landed between us. One of her hands flew up, stopping inches away from her father's face. His eyes went wide, and he halted, tipping back slightly on his heels. The fingertips of Isabel's other hand were pressed against my chest. Only a thin cotton layer separated her poison skin from mine.

My vision swirled. I slammed my eyes shut, and when I opened them a second later I saw that Isabel had taken her hand away from me.

"Where is the girl?" Isabel demanded for the third time.

Dr. Ford ignored his daughter and shouted over her to me, "I told you to stay away! It's not my fault you fail to listen. The American girl happened before you started coming around, but those other two from San Juan . . . "

"Sara!" I interrupted. "Marisol. Celia. They have names!"

"I don't care about their names." Spit flew from Dr. Ford's lips. "Isabel is *dying*. She's worth more than every one of those girls out there. I'm trying to do what's best for my daughter. Tell me that I'm wrong."

"You're wrong!"

"No." Dr. Ford extended his right arm out by his side and flipped his palm to face up. The quick movement caused his gold cufflink to glint. "Listen to me. On one side, you have Isabel." He then extended his left hand and flipped that palm. "On the other, you have all the other girls on this decaying little island, all the Marisols and Saras and Celias and on and on." The doctor paused, his mad, dark eyes shining. "Isabel is a marvel. There's no one else like her in the entire world. Her life deserves preserving."

"My *life*," Isabel sneered. She inched closer to her father, causing him to take a shaky step back and stumble over a chair. He checked his balance by clinging to the side of the table. Isabel continued to approach him, with her hand out-stretched and her fingers spread wide. "This is not a life."

Isabel was as frightening as I'd ever seen her, lean and hungry-looking. She lifted her face so the tip of her nose nearly brushed her father's chin. He turned his head slightly to the side, took in a single breath, and held it. Beads of sweat trickled down from his hairline and jaw.

"Please, Isabel," Dr. Ford begged. "I can find a way . . . I'm close. This is what you wanted."

Isabel shook her head. "Not anymore."

"I just need more time! The little one. Celia. She shows promise. There's something special about her. Her immunity . . . "

"No!" Isabel yelled. "No more time. No more girls."

"Your mother . . . "

"Don't talk about my mother!" Isabel reached down and grabbed her father's wrist. He hissed as if having been stung. "Is Celia dead or not?"

Dr. Ford swallowed, then twitched, the way a person does when he's in pain and doesn't want anyone to know. Sweat glistened on his neck, his forehead, and above his lip. After several seconds, his eyelids began to flutter. His expression went slack, and the rest of his body followed. First, his eyes rolled back into his head. His limbs drooped; his neck lost its ability to hold his head upright. His legs failed, and he began to tip forward. Isabel loosened her grip and stepped back, allowing her father's body to fall hard to the floor. His head bounced against the tile and made a sick popping sound. I flinched, but Isabel seemed not to care. She skirted around the far end of the dining room table and threw open the double doors to the courtyard, leaving me alone with the still body of her father. One of his hands was resting, palm up, on the top of my shoe.

"He's dead," I whispered.

"He's not dead," Isabel called out from the courtyard, where she'd begun to furiously rip the leaves off various plants and toss them into piles. "I had my fingers on his pulse the whole time."

I kicked away the doctor's hand and ran outside. Isabel was now tearing handfuls of leaves from the low limbs of a tree. A mosquito landed on my hand, another on my arm. I hit both them at the same time, leaving the scraps of their mangled bodies on my skin.

"This is what *you* wanted?" I demanded. "Is that what your dad said? You wanted Sara, Marisol, and Celia all dead?"

Isabel spun around and took a step in my direction. Bunches of leaves were gripped tight in her fists. The look on her face was the same as the one she'd just given her dad, bold and wild, and while I was scared of her, I knew she was scared of me, too.

"I wanted to not be sick," she said. "I wanted to get better and be normal. I was desperate. My dad said he'd found a way to help me." Her chest heaved, causing her voice to crack into a wheeze. "There's a chance that Celia might not—"

"Why Marisol?" I interrupted. "Why her?"

"Because . . . " Isabel tightened her fists, crushing the leaves within them to pulp. "Because I told him to."

Sorry, Lucas. This one I just can't grant.

I hated her. I'd never hated anyone as much as I hated Isabel in that moment.

"You knew what had happened to Marisol, and you didn't say anything."

"I was going to!" The wildness in her eyes still shone, but the boldness had faded. In its place was a mess of guilt and confusion. "That's why I sent the note about the disappeared girl, I . . . "

It was getting harder to breathe. My lungs. The air. It was what Isabel was telling me; it was Isabel; it was all the poison leaves torn from their poison stems.

I tipped my head back, looked to the still blue sky, got dizzy, slammed my eyelids shut.

"This is your fault!" I cried out.

"I know it's my fault!" Isabel sobbed. "Lucas, I'm sorry. I was scared of dying, and I was angry at being cursed, and I knew it was wrong . . . I didn't think he'd take Celia. She's so young. I was really hoping that she'd just wandered off, and that someone would find her."

I opened my eyes, slowly, and took small sips of air. "How many are there?"

Isabel shook her head, but didn't respond.

"Was Sara the first?"

"No. I don't know. I don't know how many." Isabel dropped the pulverized leaves from her fists and wiped fresh tears from her cheeks with the back of one of her green-stained hands. "He kept a lot of the details from me."

"I could say the same about you. Keeping details from me."

"I didn't know you." She paused to transfer a mix of tears and pulp from her hands onto her jeans. "I still don't. Not really. You need to get away from me. You're getting sick again."

"What are you doing with all that?" I asked, ignoring her statement and gesturing to the leaves she'd started to collect in piles.

"I'm leaving."

"Leaving to do what?"

Isabel reached out and yanked a foot-long waxy leaf from the limb the nearest plant. "To find Celia."

"No way." I shook my head. "If anyone's going after her, it's going to be me. If you know where she is, you have to tell me."

"Like you said, Lucas. This all happened because of me, and I'm the one who's going to fix it."

"You do not *fix* things, Isabel. You *destroy* them."

Isabel flinched. For a moment, she looked just like her father did earlier, teetering on the brink of collapse. But she quickly found her balance, regained what little composure she had left, and came close, too close. Her chin lifted so her nose was nearly grazing my lips.

Isabel and I knew each other more than she was willing to give us credit for, and this was her power play. Like the other night, the night of the storm, when, for just the shortest of moments, Isabel was so close I could feel her breath on my skin. Fear and desire, in equal measure, pulsed in the space between us. Isabel liked to pretend to be fearless, but she wasn't. She knew that I knew she wasn't.

"How do you plan on stopping me, Lucas?" she taunted, whisking the long leaf across my cheek. "Huh?"

"I'm not going to stop you," I said, snatching the leaf from her hand and flinging it away. "I'm coming with you. You may know where Celia is, or you may not. There's only one way for me to find out."

"You are *not* coming with me, Lucas."

"You have no idea what you're doing." I pointed past the top of her courtyard wall. "You won't last thirty minutes out there."

She opened her mouth to protest, but I cut her off. "But more than that, I don't trust you."

Isabel turned, sizing up the piles of leaves scattered around the courtyard before casting a long, melancholy glance at the inert form of her father on the floor of the dining room.

"This better not be you trying to play the hero, Lucas."

I grinned. "Better me than you, Isabel."

"You think I have no idea what *I'm* doing? *You* have no

173

idea what *you're* doing," she scoffed. "You may not last thirty minutes with me."

"It's a chance I'm willing to take. For Celia. For Marisol."

"Fine." Isabel cleared her throat. "For Celia." She gestured to the strewn leaves. "I need something to put all this in. I need a place nearby where we can go hide out for a couple of hours so I can work on something. I want to be long gone before my dad comes to. It can't be your convent. He'll go there first."

Isabel dashed through the courtyard door and over to the twisting staircase. Once there, she put her foot on the bottom step and turned toward me.

"I need you upstairs."

Isabel lived in a room of glass. If anyone were to have seen it from outside, they would've thought they were looking at a perfectly perched rooftop solarium. Rows of thick plants obscured the windows that lined the room on all four sides. I could just make out their tall shadows and hear the squeaks of their stems being dragged across the glass by the wind.

In the center of the room was a nearly rusted four-poster bed covered with a multicolored quilt and rumpled pages from old issues of *El Nuevo Día*. Stacks of books leaned against every immovable object, from the glass walls to the twin green nightstands to an armoire in the corner made of a dark-lacquered wood. Next to the armoire was a pile of canvases, and propped up against that was a folded easel. The whole place smelled like grass, oil paint, and turpentine.

Isabel yanked open the armoire doors and started tossing out clothing.

"I don't remember where I put . . . here! Hold this." She handed me a duffel bag, and then spun around to dig under the bed. Within seconds, she'd pulled out what looked like a child's plastic suitcase.

She then moved over to her desk to search through the piles of junk there, including several teacups and a mason jar full of used paintbrushes.

"What do you need me to do?" I asked.

"I'm looking for thread. Spools of thread. It doesn't matter the color. Check the trunks behind you."

I turned. Lined up against one of the glass walls were four large trunks, the kind that fill grandmothers' attics and contain costumes, old photos, and mothballs. Isabel's contained none of that. The first was stuffed with mismatched sheets and blankets; the second was empty except for a handful of buttons, a single flower, dried to black, and a pair of opera glasses. The third trunk—made of wood stained blood red— was filled almost to the top with pieces of paper of all different sizes and colors. Some were scraps: receipts, torn corners of yellow notebook paper, pieces of matchbooks. Others were bigger: sheets of tracing paper and rolls held tight with disintegrating rubber bands.

Some of the stray papers fluttered out and fell to the ground. One was a blue square, the size of a drink coaster.

My knees hurt, someone had written on it.

Another, written in crayon on a page torn from a coloring book: *Make my baby sister stop crying.*

Another, on onionskin, in peacock-blue ink so old the words had faded to illegibility. Something about a *daughter,* or maybe a *disaster.*

They were wishes. There must have been hundreds.

"You've got to be freaking kidding me," I muttered. Turning, I saw Isabel holding the little suitcase, along with the duffel and a folded white blanket. She'd thrown the hood of her sweatshirt over her head.

"You and your friends weren't the first to drop wishes over my wall," she said. "They still come, though not as often as they used to."

"Why do you keep them?"

"Because they make me feel like I'm a part of people's lives. I found the thread." She held up the suitcase. "Do you know of a place we can go?"

"Yeah," I said, closing the lid of the trunk. "I do. How long has it been since you've been to the beach?"

PART THREE

LEAVES

SEVENTEEN

MY MOM LEFT on my first day of second grade. She'd fixed me oatmeal that morning as usual, and, as usual she'd packed my lunch and put it in my backpack. After driving me the short distance to my school while we both listened to news radio, she'd waved to me as I got out of the car and was absorbed by the mass of shrieking kids.

I remember her shouting out the car window, "I'll see you later, Luke!"

At 3:45 that afternoon, my grandma—my mother's mother—drove up to the empty school in her ancient forest-green Buick. I'd been on the swings, waiting in the warm late-summer sun. The other kids were long gone. That wasn't abnormal. When my mom or dad had to work late, they'd ask my grandma to pick me up. They always told her that school let out at 3 p.m.—which was fifteen minutes earlier than school actually let out—because they knew she'd be late. The reason my grandma was always late, my dad had said, was because she had lived for so long in the Dominican Republic and that people in the Caribbean have no sense of time.

My grandma honked her horn and then stuck her whole arm out of the window to wave. She was always one to make her presence known, even if we were the only two people around. I leapt off the swings and raced to the car. Without acknowledging that she was late, my grandma drove me home. After letting us in with her spare key, she made me oatmeal—just like my mom had done that morning. While we sat at the table, I had her tell me stories I'd heard hundreds of times, stories of living in the forests outside of Santo Domingo, where the monkeys would come right up to you and snatch food from your hands if you weren't watching, and how my mom used to climb trees higher and hold her breath underwater longer than all the boys.

"You should have seen her, Lucas," my grandmother had said. "Like a deer, that girl could run—fast and graceful through the grass. No one could catch her. She would point to the highest of the mountains and tell me that she was going to live there someday."

Along with my mom, my grandma was one of the first storytellers in my life, and for a long time the Caribbean islands seemed like a land of fantasy, where myths passed for history and my mother was a marvelous daredevil, whose speed and agility was the envy of everyone.

When my dad came home in the early evening and saw my grandma and me sitting by ourselves at the kitchen table, he told me to go to my room. It was there that I saw a note from my mom on the bed. As I read it, I could hear my dad yelling from the other side of the house, saying that he should have known better and demanding information my grandma couldn't or wouldn't give.

Mom's note was written in black pen on a piece of green construction paper she'd taken from my desk. The note said that she'd never thought she was a very good mom and I'd grow up stronger without her. She told me she loved me and that even though I might be mad at her for a little while, I'd soon see that her moving away would turn out to be the best thing for the both of us. *I'm doing this for you*, she'd written. On the bottom of the page, she'd drawn a picture of a palm tree.

My dad never found out about the note. I'd hidden it in a shoebox under my bed and would only pull it out every so often. I finally threw it away a couple of years ago. I'd learned enough by then to know my mom was full of shit. She'd claimed her decision to leave had been about me and my well-being, when, in reality, it had been about her and her nagging regrets about marrying my dad, starting a family, and leaving a place where she could climb to the tops of the highest trees and swim in clear warm water. There were no mountains for her to live on in Houston.

During the cab ride east toward Condado Beach, with Isabel beside me in the backseat, I was reminded of my mom.

Something Dr. Ford had said earlier, about how marvelous Isabel was, had triggered my memory. He was acting in her best interest, he'd said; he'd been doing it all for her. Bullshit. He was doing it all for himself. Just like my mother had done. At least Isabel had the guts to own up to her atrocity. Her father had hit the floor still clinging to the belief that his actions were somehow justifiable.

"I hope you're right about this," I said.

Isabel shifted, slanting her knees away from me and toward her door. The duffel bag stuffed with stems and leaves from the plants in the Ford's courtyard was wedged between Isabel's feet, and the little green plastic suitcase sat between the two of us. Folded on Isabel's lap was the white blanket. Folded on that blanket were her hands. They trembled slightly, along with the breaths she was trying hard to keep smooth and quiet.

"I am." Isabel had her gaze directed toward the window; the hood of her sweatshirt was still up, covering most her hair, and all I could see of her face was a dim reflection in the glass. "If she's alive, she's out near Rincón, in one of my dad's cabins. I'm sure once we're out on the road, I can find them again."

I had to believe her. I had no choice. This mission was set in motion, and unless I wanted to take off by myself and search the entire island with nothing to guide me but weakly burning hope, I was forced to follow Isabel's lead.

"What is this place we're going to, exactly?" Isabel asked.

Earlier, when we'd first climbed into the cab on Calle Sol, I'd given the driver the address of the abandoned hotel on Condado Beach. He'd lowered the volume of the guajira son music that had been blaring from his speakers. His eyes had shot up to the rearview mirror and narrowed to indicate he hadn't heard me right. He blurted out a question in such rapid Spanish that the only word I could understand was "hotel." After watching me try to sort out the words of two languages in my head for a couple of seconds, Isabel answered the cab driver in Spanish. Even then he'd still seemed confused.

"De veras!" she'd exclaimed, tossing her hand in the air. That I understood. It roughly translated into, *yeah, really.*

"It's an old hotel."

"I gathered that." Isabel turned her head, which allowed me to glimpse again the iron-gray strands of hair falling from her hood and across her chest. "I guess I meant, how did you come across it?"

Isabel pulled the blanket more tightly into her lap. The bruise on her hand, the one I'd touched, was larger now, extending down toward her wrist, spreading like a blue-black rash. My kiss didn't make it better. Of course it didn't.

"Rico and Ruben and Carlos and I found it when we were kids," I replied. "Every summer when I come back to San Juan, I'm surprised it's still here."

"It's nice you've all been friends that long," she said.

I realized she was baiting me, subtly, and I didn't want

to bite. The plan was for us to get to La Andalusia and stay there until Isabel finished up whatever she needed to do. I'd find a phone, call Rico, and convince him to let us borrow his scooter. Isabel and I would head west as quickly as we could, ideally before sundown. There was no part of the plan that involved Isabel and me making small talk or getting to know each other better.

And yet. A small slice of the anger I felt towards her was softening into pity. Back in her courtyard, she'd mentioned her sorry excuse for a life, and there was no way I could argue with that. Physically, she was withering away. Her poison blood was seeping to the surface, bleaching her hair and marring her skin. She had no friends, no mother. No one had ever held her hand. Her closest companions were her plants and the desperate strangers who threw their wishes to her.

"Things will be different next year," I said. "My dad told me they're tearing the convent down. We'll be staying out at Rincón, where his firm is building a new resort. Rico and Ruben could maybe come out for a day or two, but I know once Carlos has saved enough money, he's leaving the island completely."

"Rincón is not so bad," Isabel offered. She turned again to face the window, craning her head to try and peer down the shoreline. "You think we're close?"

I pulled the sheet of plywood away from the window and followed Isabel into La Andalusia.

Once inside the old ballroom, Isabel made a beeline for one of the tables, opened her suitcase, and pulled out a small sewing machine. She stripped off her sweatshirt and then set the machine up quickly, positioning a spool of dark-colored thread on the spindle and winding it through the machine. After that, she attached a pedal, which she placed down by her feet.

"There's no electricity in here," I said, noting the coin-sized bruises that ran up and down both of her arms. "You should've told me."

She shook the leaves onto the table and unfolded the blanket. "Not a problem. The machine runs on a pedal."

I watched as she pumped the pedal with her foot and brought the machine whirring to life. I remembered the shirt she'd given me on the night of the hurricane, the one with the mend her father had recognized.

"Where'd you learn how to do this?"

Isabel yanked the black thread free from its spool and deftly wound it through the machine. "One collects these types of hobbies out of boredom and necessity."

"You're sure you won't take long?"

"I'll be as quick as I can. Don't get too close, though. When the needle pierces the leaves the smell might make your head spin."

Isabel pulled a long dollar-bill-green leaf from the pile and laid it out on top of the blanket. She then guided both of the layers through the machine. She did the same thing with another long leaf and another section of the blanket. When she reached the bottom, she pivoted the short end of the blanket and started going up the way she'd come.

After pacing for close to ten minutes, I went across the room and collapsed on a couch, the same one I'd slept on the night I found Marisol. I shut my eyes and draped my arm across them, attempting to block out my senses, maybe even get lucky enough to snag some rest. Instead, I was plagued by the torturous humming of Isabel's machine. The persistent needle went up and down in a quick, determined rhythm. My watch, inches from my ear, ticked slowly and surely. My heart, however, bucked erratically. My mind raced.

"Tell me about Zabana," I demanded, my eyes still closed.

Isabel hesitated. "How do you know her name?"

"Your dad brought over one of his books to the hotel. He dedicated it to her. He wrote that nothing could tear them apart. But something obviously did."

I opened my eyes and turned my head toward Isabel—the very something—that was able to tear apart Zabana and Rupert.

"Did she leave because you were sick?" I asked. "That seems like a pretty shitty thing to do."

"She was ashamed." Isabel cast a quick glance up to me. "I am the way I am because of her. She felt like leaving was her only option—at least that's what she told my dad."

Isabel plucked a leaf from her pile and readied for another pass through the machine.

"She took the bird and left a curse," I said. "That's what the señoras always said."

"Why are you bringing this up? Isabel asked wearily. "Truly, you don't care about me or my mother or . . . "

"I need a distraction," I replied, cutting Isabel off. "Please. Just talk. I need a story to distract me from the ones that I'm currently making up in my head about Celia dead in some cabin in the middle of the forest. Silence isn't doing me any good right now."

Isabel's eyes shot up to mine again. They examined me the same way they'd done the first day I landed in her courtyard—warily — like she wasn't sure she approved of what she saw.

"The señoras weren't completely wrong," she said after a beat. "The story goes that my mom was a jíbara, a peasant. She grew up in a tiny beach village on the south side of the island, outside of Ponce. One afternoon when she was fifteen years old, she was out on the water's edge weaving together a small basket from strips of fallen palm fronds when a man approached her. He spoke in a language she'd never heard before, but she somehow understood him. After giving her a warning about a boy with a scar on his right cheek who would grow up to destroy the village, he took the strips of the fronds out of her hands and wove a perfect basket, just big enough to hold three swallows of water.

"My mom was scared because her brother Tino had a scar on his right cheek," Isabel continued. "Even though she loved him very much and he'd been the one to teach her how to swim and write and draw pictures, she went back to her village to show her mother her basket and pass on the warning from the man. Once she heard the story, my grandmother led my mom to the hut where the cacique lived. There, she repeated what happened to her, word for word, to the old lady with the gray eyes and tangled gray hair who she'd been afraid of her whole life. The cacique offered my mom some water and a piece of bread and touched her lightly on her arm. She asked what exactly my mom was doing when the man appeared. She wanted to know exactly what he looked like and what he said."

"Wait," I said, staring up at the water-stained ceiling. "What's a cacique?"

"A cacique's a Taíno chieftain," Isabel replied. "She leads the community. Anyway, my mom ate the bread, told the cacique what she'd been doing, what the man had looked like, and what he'd said. The old lady then patted my mom on the head and told her she was very brave. That night, four men came to my mom's family's house and took Tino away. As he was being dragged through the door, he placed a curse on my mother. He said that he hoped her belly would be full of poison and that any of her children and her children's children would die in the streets like dogs. My mom stood frozen and said nothing. She said she could feel his words. They landed all over her body, and like worms, they burrowed through her skin and into her organs.

"The next morning the cacique told my mom she was a bohique—a priestess—and the man she had spoken to on the beach was a god. He'd come to give her a message because he knew she was one of the few people who could receive it. Because of that message, the cacique said, my mom saved many lives."

Isabel paused briefly. "Of course there was never any proof of that. My dad has told me this story dozens of times, and he always stops right here and snorts and says, 'Of course there was never any proof of that.'"

"Regardless . . . " Isabel sighed. "The cacique told my grandma that her daughter was a rare gift to her people, but my mom never believed it; what she *did* believe was that Tino cursed her and that she could feel that curse festering inside her belly."

Even though Isabel had lied to me in a variety of unforgivable ways, I believed this story. It was about magic and disappearing. Zabana was special, but her village eventually forgot her. Then it forgot itself. I thought about my mother again, though this time about the story of la ciguapa with the backward feet, and then her asking me: *What's there not to believe?*

"According to my dad, the world spun very quickly in the following years," Isabel said. "The island got bigger and smaller at the same time. People starting moving out of their villages to the bigger cities, like Ponce and San Juan, and my mom stopped going to the beach where the god had woven the basket for her. The cacique died, and no one replaced her. In addition to Borinquen, my mom learned to speak both Spanish and English. She dreamed of moving away.

"She and my dad met when she was still a teenager. She'd taken a trip to Ponce with a boy she'd pretended to like, but really she was just using him for his car. They'd gone to a bar, and that's where she'd seen my dad, with his lighter brown hair and a suit she thought was too old-fashioned. When my dad told my mom he was a scientist, that he'd come to the island to study its tropical plants, she told him about how, when she was a little girl, she would weave bowls out of palm fronds."

"My dad always claimed he loved my mom madly, but she told him she thought that he loved her like an imperialist would, that he found her 'exotic' or 'curious.' After all, she was just a jíbara from a tiny beach village, who'd grown up with next to nothing and whose parents worked in sugar fields and died too young. He swore up and down that wasn't the case. The word he'd used to describe her all those warm nights they'd kissed under the swaying trees was 'magical.' My dad would say to me, 'Isa, you are magical just like your mother.'"

There was a hitch in Isabel's voice, either from being overwhelmed by emotion or from trouble with her breathing. She paused before gathering her waves of hair into a thick coil and tossing it over one shoulder.

"My dad still won't believe in the curse. I know he loved

my mom very much, but he never understood. He's a scientist. He'll always try to find the most logical solution. That's why we're here right now."

"We're here right now," I said, "because of how petty and jealous you are."

The needle on Isabel's machine to screeched to a halt.

"We're here *right now*," Isabel repeated, "because of how petty and jealous I am. You're right. And I haven't forgotten about that for a *single* second. I've avoided telling you about my mother because I haven't wanted to shift blame onto her, or her curse, or her brother, or my father, or whoever or whatever."

Isabel was scowling, her bony shoulders hitched up by her ears. Her rickety frame looked like it held a world of damage and pain, like it had been patched up and reglued countless times.

"You never found out what happened to your mom?"

"What's to find out, Lucas?" Isabel asked, exasperated. "She's gone, desaparecida. When I was a kid, my dad used to take me with him as he searched the island for my mother. He made it all the way to the village near Ponce where she was born. He told me later that all he found there was an empty village, a deaf old man, and his three-legged dog. There weren't even any houses left." She glared at me. "What about *your* mom? She's desaparecida, too, right?"

Stung, I turned onto my back and closed my eyes. "Yeah, she's . . . *gone*."

A couple of seconds ticked away. "That's it?"

Of course that wasn't *it*, but what little of my mother I had, I liked to keep to myself. The thing was, Isabel and I were the same this way. The two of us clung to the scraps of stories that when cobbled together made a strange and incomplete picture of a parent.

"She grew up in the Dominican Republic," I began. "She was adopted by a couple of white doctors who worked with poor people out in the countryside. When she was my age, she went away to boarding school and then college in Texas. She met my dad there. They got married, had me. She moved to New York when I was ten. We lost touch. End of story."

"I would have never have guessed you were Dominican," Isabel said. Her machine clicked and whirred back to life. "You look just like your dad."

"If you saw pictures, you'd think I looked just like my mom. She had blonde hair and blue eyes. She never knew who her real parents were, and my grandma never talked about it."

"Does she have a new family?"

"As far as I know she's alone."

"So, that's where you get your solitary nature from."

I barked out a laugh. "When I was a kid, I dreamed of living here in this building. I thought there was no way I'd ever get tired of finding new places to explore and to hide in."

"It's a good place," Isabel said. "If I wasn't the way I am

I could live here. I'd mostly keep to myself, except for once a year when I'd have a party. I'd invite the entire island. There'd be music and dancing. I'd wear a dress, a long, sparkling green dress with no sleeves. That way the people, when they passed me, might skim up against my bare skin. And on that one night I would turn on all the lights in the building, and it would be so bright that sailors miles away could see it."

Isabel stopped talking, so I opened my eyes and turned to see why. She'd hit a snag and was hunched over the machine, her nose scrunched up and the tip of her tongue pushing past her teeth as she concentrated on untangling a mess of thread and plant fibers.

It was all so real. Isabel wasn't a myth. A myth is simple. Isabel was a muddled mess. Like Marisol, she had big, impossible dreams. Like me, she was teetering on a line between bending to the will of her father and piloting her own future. She was just a girl trying to make a blanket out of leaves. In that moment, it seemed perfectly within the bounds of normalcy.

"I guess for someone who's spent most of her life creeping around in the shadows it makes sense you'd want to be the center of the attention every now and then," I offered.

"Oh no, Lucas." Isabel shook her head and glanced up. "You don't understand. The party wouldn't be for me. It would be for the island."

Isabel eventually got her snag straightened out, and the regular humming of the sewing machine eventually lulled me to sleep. That's when I dreamed of the real Isabel for the first time—no green skin, no grass for hair. She was at her party at La Andalusia. The ballroom looked like I'd always thought it should've: lit up brilliantly by its massive chandelier, filled with men wearing stiff black suits and beautiful women wearing long slinky dresses that clung to their legs when they walked and spun around. The partygoers all stood and laughed and danced on carpet that was as red as blood from a freshly pricked finger. As they raised their glasses to their lips, the crystal winked.

Small leaves, brittle and brown, dotted the carpet. They swirled around the ankles of dancing couples and were crushed under sharp heels and slick soles of leather shoes.

Isabel was in the center of the room, laughing and surrounded by her guests. She wore a dark green strapless dress that fell down to her feet, and her hair was pulled up in a bun that sat just above the nape of her neck. Two chunky wooden bracelets hung around her right wrist. Her skin glowed in the near-blinding light.

I looked to the mirror behind the bar and saw that I was dressed like the other men, in a black suit and bow tie against a white dress shirt. My hair was slicked back and so appeared darker than normal. Silver cufflinks glinted at my wrists. The glasses hanging above the bar and the liquor bottles on the shelf were starting to rattle from chamber music that was getting louder and louder. No one seemed to hear the music except for me.

Above my head, the chandelier pulsed and shook, its individual crystals crashing against each other.

I panicked and pushed through the crowd, calling out Isabel's name. Either she couldn't hear me or was choosing not to respond. She was laughing; everyone was laughing. She raised her champagne flute into the air; everyone raised their champagne flutes into the air. When she made her way up to each of her guests and rested her hand gently on their shoulder or caressed their cheek with her fingertips, they gave her that look of reverence and gratitude usually reserved for someone holy. They were there just for her.

However.

Mere seconds after Isabel touched a woman's shoulder or caressed a man's face, that person would stop laughing, and their smile would fade. They would stumble off and put their glass down on the edge of a table. They checked their balance against a chair or another person before falling to the ground. Even though the partygoers were collapsing on top of one another in piles, more women in long slinky dresses and men in black suits took their place, lined up for Isabel.

I shoved my way through the crowd, but it kept expanding. Some faces belonged to strangers, but others I recognized. There was Señora Garcia, the old lady who lived on Calle Sol. She was standing on the far side of the room next to a one-eyed man who worked at one of the food stalls at the market and who was always fingering the crucifix that hung against his breastbone. Near them was my dad, in a light blue suit and Panama hat. The older Reyes women were in a corner, a chorus of mourning in black veils. A single candle in a votive made of red glass was resting in the center of each of their open palms. They were calling out to me, but I couldn't hear what they were saying over the music and sounds of clinking glass.

A girl called out my name. I knew it was Marisol before I even turned. She was with Celia; they were holding hands. They were soaking wet. Their hair was long, too long. It came down to their ankles. They started walking toward me, and it was then I saw their feet—heels forward, toes pointing back. They opened their mouths as if to sing but nothing came out.

I took a step toward them, but then, in an instant, everyone vanished. It was just me and Isabel and the long and layered notes of stringed instruments. As I walked up to her, she latched onto my wrist, pulled me toward her, and pressed her lips against mine.

I kissed her. I didn't want to, but I had to. She was hurting me, but I wanted her to hurt me more. Her mouth tasted like ash. I closed my eyes. I wrapped my fingers around her shoulders and could feel her bones breaking under the skin and thin muscle. My fingers reached down to hers, causing them to snap. She wanted me to hold her close, but all my hands and lips found was a body that was disintegrating like dried paper.

I opened my eyes, and the music finally stopped. Isabel was gone, leaving me grasping at stale air. The chandelier above my head was still and blooming with light. I was alone in the beautiful ruin of La Andalusia, like I'd always loved to be, with tiny brown leaves swirling around my feet.

EIGHTEEN

I WOKE WITH a start and a bar of sun across my face. I sat up and looked around the room, running my fingernails across my scalp and trying to smack the taste of sleep out of my mouth. When I squinted at my watch I saw it was 11:35, a little over three hours since we'd first left Isabel's house. I remembered the Celia from my dream—monstrous, soaked, and silently screaming—and jumped to my feet. I called out Isabel's name and was met with echoes.

Isabel's sewing machine was packed back up in its suitcase. The table she'd been working at was empty, and the chair she'd been sitting on was neatly pushed in. Isabel was nowhere in sight.

I stepped across the faded red carpet and crawled through the open window, emerging into the balmy, mosquito-plagued morning and onto a deserted beach. Isabel was down by the water's edge. Her back was turned toward me. She'd taken off her jeans and was wearing just her white cotton tank top and what looked like black underwear. She'd gathered her hair into a bun at the nape of her neck, just like in my dream. Without her clothes on and without her hair flowing around her shoulders, she looked shockingly small.

If things were different, if she had just been a girl I knew, if there had been no Marisol, this might have happened: I might've walked up behind her and threaded my arms around her waist. She might've lifted her head up, tilted it back. We'd have kissed. Her lips would've been warm.

I shook off the image before it was fully formed. It wasn't fair to Isabel to imagine her as any different than biology and a curse had created her.

I called out her name, and she turned. Wisps of loose hair blew around her face while the small frothy waves broke around her ankles. With the rays of the sun coming up over her shoulder, she smiled in that wry way a person smiles when they're hiding a secret. I kicked off my Converse, rolled up the cuffs of my jeans, and ran out toward her.

"It's been forever since I've been on a beach," she said, licking her dry lips.

We stood for a moment, side by side, as if considering the wonder of the sun.

"This is near where you found Marisol."

I pointed off to my left. "Just down there."

The police tape from that night was long gone. Waves innocently lapped against the shore. The beach had tucked the memory of Marisol away in its depths and forgotten her.

A small surge rose up around our ankles, and Isabel kicked lightly at the surf with her left foot.

"We should go."

"You can stay a little while longer," I offered. "I've got to find a phone and call Rico."

Isabel turned. Her black eyes lingered on my face so long I had to look away. Down the beach a golden-haired dog, most likely a stray, barked as it tried to snatch up water in its jaws.

"I know you hate me," she said. "I can figure out a way to do this without you."

"No you can't," I replied. "Just promise me this plan of yours will actually work. I'm having a hard time believing your dad would've come back to San Juan and left Celia out there somewhere by herself."

Isabel looked back to the ocean. "It's what he's done with me practically all of my life. Since I was younger than Celia."

"Why would he come back, though?"

In front of us, a seagull soared in a circle over the water before halting, tucking its wings, and diving for a fish.

"I'm not sure," Isabel replied. "You saw him. He left in a hurry. He may have forgotten something."

Maybe. But I had the suspicion there had to be something else—something about why he came back when he did, why I found him drinking scotch in the library of the St. Lucia, why he gave me that book and talked openly about being my mentor, why he was roaming around the festival.

I searched Isabel's face for telltale signs of lying—a jaw

held tight, the unnecessary tucking of hair behind her ear—but she was simply looking out into the sea as if searching it for ships.

"We should go," she repeated, more urgently this time.

I turned and started trudging through the sand toward the hotel. Once I reached my shoes, I glanced back to the water. The sun continued to beat down against the beach, but there wasn't a small-framed, dark-haired girl basking in it anymore. Then a head broke the surface of the water far from the shore. As soon as it appeared it disappeared again, and a moment later Isabel's feet kicked up from the waves, as if she were diving straight down in an attempt touch the bottom of the ocean.

The nearest phone was at the front desk of one of the neighboring high-rise hotels. Rico was pissed that I'd woken him up, but when I told him it was an emergency and I needed him to get to La Andalusia, he said to give him ten minutes. I'd left out as many details as I could, which was easy because Rico rarely asked for specifics about anything.

As I was making my way back through the lobby, I noticed a small crowd gathered near the bar, watching a special news report on one of the screens. There was a grainy picture of Celia. Under that was the number for a tip line.

"Poor girl," I heard someone murmur. "I hope they catch the creep who did this."

"Again, to revisit our top story," said the newscaster.

"Police are searching for a possible suspect in the case of the disappearance of Celia Reyes. Sources confirm that suspect's name as Michael Lucas Knight, aged seventeen."

My yearbook picture appeared on the screen. It was followed by a live shot of Detective Lopez. Several microphones surrounded her crimson lips.

"A mentor of Mr. Knight," she said, "a man who lives on Calle Sol in the old city who wishes to remain nameless at this time, claims that Lucas confessed his crimes to him. After that confession, and when the older man threatened to call the police, Mr. Knight attacked him and left him for dead."

I squinted, and cocked my head like a man who's just been hanged. There I was, onscreen. There were words coming out of Mara Lopez's mouth. None of it made sense.

A voice from off screen demanded, "Are we to assume that the Reyes cases are now linked?"

Detective Lopez turned to share a glance with the tall, thin man next to her. I remembered him but not his name. He'd also interviewed me the night I found Marisol.

"All we're willing to say is that Mr. Knight is a 'person of interest,' and that while we're asking for the public's help in finding him, we also ask that they be careful. His mentor claims Mr. Knight stole a firearm from his house. It's also important to note that the young man does have a history with the San Juan Police Department."

Sensing eyes on me, I looked down to my left. There, a little girl with blonde hair in two perfect pigtails was holding a beach towel and staring up at me. With her free hand, she slowly reached up to tug on her dad's shirt.

I ran.

NINETEEN

I BOLTED INTO La Andalusia, where Isabel was sitting on the floor near her suitcase. Her wet hair was twisted up in a knot, and the hood of her sweatshirt was again thrown over her head.

"Your dad," I gasped. "They're showing my picture on the news."

Isabel sprang to her feet and rushed to look out the window. "Did anyone see you?"

"No. Yes." I shook my head and doubled over, bracing my hands on my knees. "I don't know. A little girl, maybe."

I heard the distinctive whine and sputter of Rico's scooter approaching.

"He's been setting me up this whole time!" There was that feeling again, in my throat and in my lungs, as if they were being forced to suck in bad air. "He took Marisol and Celia, knowing I was connected to them. He told my dad he was my mentor and all about my newfound interest in poisonous plants. Then he went and told Mara Lopez—who *hates* me—that I confessed to him and then left him for dead."

I looked up and saw Isabel, pacing, gnawing on the edge of a blackened thumbnail.

"Please tell me you didn't know about this," I begged. "Because if you're lying, this is finished. I'm leaving you here to haunt this place by yourself, and I'm going out to find Celia."

"No!" Isabel cried out. "I knew he was taking the girls, but I didn't know he was trying to frame you for it. Lucas, I promise."

"Why Marisol, then?" I demanded. "Out of all the girls, why did you pick her?"

Isabel faltered. "She had a wish to throw," she said. "She had you."

The very next moment, Rico climbed through the open window and stumbled into the room.

"Shit, man," he chuckled. "I don't remember that hole being so small."

Rico surveyed the room, but the moment he saw Isabel, he recoiled, his fingers flying up to grasp to his St. Anthony medallion.

"Who's this?"

"Have you seen the news?" I asked.

"I woke up. I came here," Rico replied flatly. He jabbed the pointer finger of the hand that wasn't twisting his charm at Isabel. "Who *is* this?"

Isabel's arms were hanging down at her sides, and her hands were clenching in and out of fists.

"This is Isabel," I said. "She lives at the house at the end of Calle Sol. She's the scientist's daughter."

Rico opened his mouth, but his voice got caught in his throat. He took a step back, and his right knee buckled. He managed to catch himself by latching on to the back of a chair with his free hand. The other was still at his throat, clutching his small token of protection. He gaped—mouth open, mouth closed—like a fish, hooked and hoisted out of the water.

After a moment, he managed to compose himself enough to let out a tiny burst of laughter. "She's not real."

I looked to Isabel. I thought her face would've shown sorrow—at the very least mild disappointment—but it was composed, as if Rico's reaction wasn't unexpected.

"Of course she's real."

"Touch her then," he dared.

I hesitated. "I can't."

"He can't," Isabel echoed.

"Why not?"

I didn't have time to get into the complexities of Isabel's existence.

"Mara Lopez is on TV," I said, "telling the entire island that I beat up Isabel's dad and kidnapped Celia."

"Why would she say that?" Rico asked.

"My dad's been taking the girls." Isabel stepped forward. "Sara, Marisol, Celia. That's why Lucas asked you to come. We need your scooter. I know where Celia is."

"If you know where Celia is, you call the cops," Rico replied, "not me."

"Are you listening?" I hissed. "The cops think I did it! Isabel's dad knew I had a history with the police here. He knew that these were Lopez's cases. He's been setting me up and steering her in my direction this *entire* time."

Rico scoffed. "Get real, Luke."

"Get real?" I moved toward him. "I'm the perfect fall guy. I'm sure half this town is already convinced I'm guilty and they're glad about it. Even Ruben turned against me."

"She came to you, too, yeah?" Rico asked with a snicker. "In your dreams? That girl whispered in your ear and told you she could give you anything you wanted? Because that's what she told me. I tried to tell her I didn't want nothing to do with her and her witchcraft, but she wouldn't listen." He ripped his hand from his pendant and flung his finger in Isabel's direction. "Whatever she promises you, Lucas, it's not worth it."

"She didn't promise me anything," I replied, pushing his hand out of the air. "Are you even listening? This is not some dream you had. This is real. *She* is real. Her dad killed Marisol and then he took Celia."

Then, coming from the direction of Avenida Ashford: the

wail of police sirens. More than one, from the sound of it. I waited for the bouncing echoes to fade away, but they only seemed to get louder.

Isabel ran over to her duffle, dug quickly through its contents, and pulled out a bundle of letters tied together with red yarn. Walking up to Rico, she held the letters out to him. As always, she'd taken the precaution of covering much of her hand with the sleeve of her sweatshirt.

"These belong to you," she said.

I knew immediately what they were. Wishes. Way more than I had ever thought to throw.

Rico waited a moment before snatching the batch of papers from Isabel and breaking the yarn. His eyes scanned the various scraps. From the size of the stack, there must have been at least twenty. Finally, his eyes lingered on one in particular. It was on a yellowed piece of lined paper, the kind with a combination of dashed and lined rows that kids use when they're learning to write cursive.

The sirens outside had grown to a near-deafening howl.

"You were younger," Rico said, his eyes still scanning his wishes. "In my dreams, you were a little girl with green skin and green hair. Your eyes are the same, though. Their color. Lucas may be right. Maybe you are real, but you're still terrifying."

Rico looked up. His mouth was closed but moving; he was chewing on his thoughts, trying to separate them out.

"I'll help you because of Celia, alright? I'm not doing this for *her*." Rico tipped his head in Isabel's direction. "You really think you're the ones who can make things right?"

Isabel nodded. "I do."

I nodded, too, accepting this strange alliance once again.

"If that's the case," Rico said, handing me his keys, "Vayan con Dios, you two. And try not to fuck up my scooter."

TWENTY

THERE WAS A wall of traffic in front of us, cars and more cars in an unbroken, unmoving chain. Sweat trailed down the sides of my face, and the fumes were making me dizzy. At least I hoped it was the fumes that were making me dizzy and not the girl huddled up behind me who'd remained quiet, her blanket of leaves barely keeping her alive and barely protecting me.

I snapped my head to the right, then the left to try and relieve the stress in my neck. This wasn't my first go-round on Rico's scooter. I'd ridden it through the bumpy, narrow streets of Old San Juan countless times, dodging cats and tourists and nearly wiping out on slick spots left by leaky jalopies. Weaving through bumper-to-bumper traffic couldn't be too different from that, right? At least the highway was somewhat evenly paved, unlike the roads in the old town. At least it wasn't raining.

The guy next to us in a rusted-out Nissan Stanza looked

from Isabel, wrapped in her blanket in eighty-five-degree weather, to me, now wearing Rico's baseball cap and denim jacket in a pathetic attempt at a disguise. His left eye twitched slightly.

"Hold on!" I yelled, revving the engine.

The scooter shot through the narrow gap between the two cars in front of us. I felt Isabel clutch at my belt loops and pull herself closer to me as drivers started honking their horns. All around us the quick beats of salsa music, the running commentary from that day's baseball game, and exhaust fumes poured from cars. We sped past a series of strange, blurry scenes: children having tantrums while tethered to their seats, a woman simultaneously eating an orange while applying mascara, a couple ferociously making out in the backseat of a taxi while the driver in the front seat spied on them in his rearview mirror, his teeth clamped together in a gross grin.

If I kept my eyes on the road ahead, I did fine. There were a few close calls when I had to swerve around cars that merged without regard for who or what they might be merging into.

After nearly fifteen minutes of mild terror, and by some miracle without running into any cops, we made it out of San Juan and were on the narrow highway heading west to Rincón.

Puerto Rico is shaped like a finger on a left hand, held to the side, and cut off at the knuckle joint. San Juan is on the northern edge, near what would be the nail bed. Rincón is on the shorter western edge, where the digit would've been severed. To get to Rincón, you have to trace the outer northern coastline until it dips south. There were other smaller roads that crosshatched the island, but they led to forests, mountains, rivers, lakes, and other out-of-the-way places people rarely went, probably for good reason.

Despite its lurking mystery, the countryside was stunning. Outside of the city, Puerto Rico was practically prehistoric. Everything was green and wide and very tall. On the side of the road, multicolored birds perched on fallen trees, and if I listened hard enough I could hear the tiny tree frogs croaking out a sound that was impossibly loud for creatures their size. Aside from the paved road and the occasional food stand or road sign, everything appeared untouched by human hands. I'd been out this way several times, but never in the open air like this—with the hot wind tearing at the folds of my clothes, the smell of the sea in my nose, and my heart beating wildly against my ribs.

I pulled over to a gas station and fruit stand just outside of a small town called Arecibo. I was anxious about stopping but also thankful for the short break. It gave me time to stretch my legs, and even with the blanket and several layers of clothes as buffers, being so close to Isabel had started to make my head spin.

A handful of tourists from the mainland were there, leaning against their cars, shaking the pebbles from their sandals, talking loudly in English, taking long pulls from bottles of water, and swatting at the air with makeshift paper fans. A mother slapped a little boy's arm to kill a mosquito and then doused him in bug repellant.

A bus from Mayagüez, a largish city south of Rincón, pulled up at the same time we did. As the passengers climbed off, many of them yawned, raising their stiff arms skyward, before heading to the stand to buy coconut water and ripe guavas.

It was a lazy scene, one that didn't fit with the emotional mess I'd become ever since leaving La Andalusia.

"I don't want to be around all these people," Isabel declared as I rode up to one of the pumps and killed the engine.

"Let me just get gas, some water, and something to eat, and then I'll move the scooter over there." I pointed to a patch of grass on the opposite side of the road.

Isabel watched as a family, including a little boy about five or six, climbed out of the car next to us. The boy had a blue blanket that was tied in a knot at his throat and draped over his shoulders. When he saw Isabel, with her blanket pulled tight around her body, he smiled broadly, held his arms out, and flexed his biceps. Isabel brought one of her arms out from under her blanket and mimicked the boy's gesture.

"He thinks you're a superhero," I said once the boy had followed his mother over to the fruit stand.

Without responding, Isabel shook her blanket off her

shoulders. She folded it and placed it under the seat along with the rest of her stuff.

I rushed to pump the gas, stop off at the restroom to splash water on my grit-covered face, and grab us a couple bottles of water and two large hunks of mango dashed with chile powder. Then I moved the scooter to the other side of the road.

"We should keep going," Isabel said, leaning against the scooter.

"We need to eat," I replied. "You also need to tell me exactly where it is we're headed."

Isabel took the mango from me and nibbled at the flesh while looking down the road and trying to reconstruct a map of the island from memory.

"Once we turn to the south, there'll be a sign for Aguadilla. A little ways after that there'll be a dirt road—or at least it was a dirt road seven years ago. We'll turn onto that and follow it for a mile or two. It'll lead to a clearing and a cabin."

That meant we'd have to take one of the snaky roads into the heart of the island after all.

"He has two cabins he uses as field labs," Isabel added. "That one's closest. The other is farther west."

"Seven years. That was the last time you were out here?"

Isabel nodded, wiping the pink juice from her mouth with the back of her hand. She pitched the thin rind into the grass behind her and looked up at me. What she asked next threw me for a loop.

"Do you know what you want to do with your life?"

I swallowed the piece of fruit I'd been chewing. "Presuming I don't wind up in jail?"

"Presuming that, yes."

"I want to live out here. I'll probably end up working for my dad."

"Don't you want to go to college? Join the military? See the rest of the world?"

I shrugged. "Not really."

"You really just want to bum around the island?" A blast of warm wind hit us like a gut punch, throwing me off balance and sending the strands of Isabel's hair in all directions. From somewhere nearby, a bird let out a long lonesome cackle. "I don't believe you."

"What's not to believe?" I tossed my own rind into the tall grass beside me and poured some of the bottled water over my arms to rinse off the sticky juice. "Why are we even talking about this?"

Isabel looked away.

"If you're thinking now is a good time for us to interview one another," I said, "I've got a few questions of my own."

"Oh, yeah?" she snapped. "Like what?"

"You were outside your house this morning. Where had you been?"

"Your room."

I choked out a laugh. "How is that possible? I would've seen you coming through the lobby or up the stairs. I was there the same time you were."

"I'm not a vampire who turns to mist," Isabel said, brushing away the hair that had blown into her face. "You have a habit of leaving your balcony doors unlocked. And climbing a palm tree to reach a second story isn't particularly difficult, even for me."

"What were you doing there?"

"I was leaving you a note. I thought I'd never see you again."

That was why no one in the hotel ever saw Isabel. She didn't slip notes under my door; she came in from the balcony and placed her notes where I was sure to find them.

Isabel looked to the ground and started tracing a wide circle in the dirt with the toe of her sneaker. She tilted her head, and over her shoulder, I spotted an old woman sitting on a bench near the fruit stand, staring straight at us.

"I don't know why people throw their wishes over my wall," Isabel said, locking her eyes with mine, "but they do. I don't know why I started showing up in people's dreams, but I did." She paused. "Did you ever dream about me?"

"All the time."

"What did I look like?"

"A little girl with green skin and grass for hair." I didn't mention the Isabel from the other dream, the one who both adored and destroyed the people around her.

"Why is that?" Isabel urged.

"Why is *what*?"

"Why do I show up in people's dreams like that? And if I'm some sort of little green monster, why do people send *me*—of *all* people—their wishes as if I had any power to grant them."

"Maybe . . . " I trailed off.

"Maybe *what*, Lucas?"

"Maybe . . . " I paused, knowing that Isabel wasn't going to like what I was about to suggest, " . . . it had something to do with your mom being able to talk to gods."

"*What?*"

"From the story you told me. Your mom talked to a god. She was a prophet or something." Isabel covered her face with her hands and groaned. "Just listen. I agree with your dad about one thing, Isabel. You're pretty . . . *unique*. Which isn't to say you're not extremely flawed in many, *many* ways, but he's right that there's no one else like you. Maybe part of that comes from your mom, but most of it is just . . . who you are."

"I'm dying, Lucas."

It was the first time I'd heard her say those words. And the way she said them, with such certainty and pity, as if I should've known this was the case since the day we met, made me feel like a fool.

I lamely pointed to the scooter seat. "What about that?"

"What *about* that?"

"The blanket. It doesn't help?"

I knew the blanket didn't help; I knew it the second the question left my lips.

"All that does is buy us the tiniest sliver of time." Isabel impatiently whipped a strand of hair behind her ear. "Can you get me another bottle of water? Maybe two so we can take one on the road? We've wasted enough time here."

That was it. Isabel had put an end to the conversation, so I hustled back over to the fruit stand and stood in line to buy water as the group from Mayagüez was starting to file back onto their bus. From inside the small stand, salsa music, punctuated by bursts of static, blasted from an old, rabbit-eared radio.

I glanced back at Isabel, who was leaning against the scooter, her eyes fixed on the road that led west. She was biting her thumbnail, but then stopped to swat at her ear with her right hand—once, twice—like a bee had flown too close.

As I came to the front of the line the music from the radio faded out and was replaced by the voice of a man speaking Spanish in a rapid clip. Because of the terrible reception, I could only make out a few words:

" . . . chica desaparecida . . . Lina Gutierrez . . . de la comunidad del Hato Rey, San Juan . . . tiene ocho años . . . "

Those garbled fragments were from a report about an eight-year-old named Lina Gutierrez, who'd gone missing from the San Juan neighborhood of Hato Rey. I thought of the little girl I'd seen Dr. Ford crouched in front of at the festival, the one with the ribbon.

Then, from the radio: "Michael Lucas Knight . . . la policía esta buscando en la vecindad de Bayamón . . . "

Bayamón? Bayamón is a town back near San Juan, nearly fifty miles away from Arecibo.

Why would the police be searching there?

I threw down my cash and grabbed the bottles of water. I turned to run back to Isabel, but was forced to stop. Someone had a hold of my sleeve. I spun around and saw the old woman from the bench—the one who had been staring at me and Isabel—standing in front of me.

She was half my height and was wearing a purple cotton dress dotted with tiny red flowers. Her hair was cut short like a boy's, and a network of deep creases crossed her face. The way she was squinting up into my face, with scrutiny and distrust, I was certain she'd recognized me from the news, but I soon saw that her eyes were so cloudy with cataracts she must've been nearly blind. Her lips curled back to reveal a toothless mouth. She was so ancient, I couldn't tell if she was smiling or grimacing.

"Si, señora?" I asked.

"Es para ella." Her voice screeched painfully, like hinges in desperate need of grease.

The old woman put one clawlike hand over her brow in an attempt to block out the sun. With her other hand, she started jabbing me in the stomach with a folded piece of paper. She motioned with her head over my shoulder toward where Isabel was waiting with the scooter. When I took the paper from her gnarled fingers and started to unfold it, the woman slapped my hand.

"No te miras! Es para ella." *Don't look,* she commanded. *It's for her.*

"Okay, okay. Lo siento. I'm sorry, señora."

The woman accepted my apology with a grunt. I watched her turn and begin hobbling over to the bus before I ran back across the road.

Isabel was still chewing on the edge of her nail, and her expression was grim. When I was close enough, she snatched the señora's paper out of my hand and read it quickly. I glanced behind me and watched the bus from Mayagüez pull away. Through one of the back windows, the woman stared at us with her blind eyes.

"That old señora thinks you're real," I said. Isabel scoffed.
"What does that say?"

She handed me the paper, on which was written a single sentence in Spanish. The handwriting was slanted and shaky; the spelling wasn't perfect, but it said something about a grandson and a doctor.

"She wants her grandson to become a doctor," Isabel clarified, retrieving her blanket of leaves and wrapping it tightly around her shoulders. "You should've told her I have no control over that."

"Why would she give you this? How could she even see you? She was practically blind. Do you know her?"

"How would I know her?" Isabel grabbed the bottles of water from my hand, stashed them under the seat, and hopped onto the scooter. "She's from Mayagüez. I've never been there in my life. Come on."

She knocked on the seat in front of her with her knuckles. I climbed on and started up the engine.

"While I was in line I heard something on the radio about a missing eight-year-old from Hato Rey," I shouted over my shoulder. "The announcer said my name. I'm a suspect in that now, too. The thing is, I'm pretty sure he also said that the police were searching near Bayamón."

"That's back near the city," Isabel replied.

"I know."

"This means Celia's alive. My dad might've given the police a bad lead and thrown them off your trail. He knew we'd come out to Rincón. I'm sure he doesn't want to lead the authorities right out to where he has Celia. If she was dead and he'd dumped her somewhere, he'd have nothing left to hide."

"Or the police assume we're listening to the radio, and they're throwing us bad leads." I revved the scooter's engine. "Mara Lopez isn't stupid."

"We have to go," Isabel urged. "Quickly. I'll bet my dad has taken this new girl and is headed back to Rincón. He won't abandon the experiment as long as he can find girls to experiment on. And when those experiments fail, he'll find a way to keep pinning the blame on you as long as you're free."

The scooter's tires kicked up dirt as I pulled out into the road.

"I said *quickly*, Lucas," Isabel shouted over the motor. "There's going to be a storm soon."

I looked to the sky for any indication of an oncoming storm, but found none. The weather was clear, and there was not a single cloud in sight. The lightest of breezes came through, carrying with it the smell of salt water.

TWENTY-ONE

A FEW MILES outside of Arecibo, the landscape started to ripple gently; then it rose and fell like two great tides. The chirps of the tiny tree frogs and the cackles of tropical birds, once soothing, were now roars and shrieks. The clear sky above was puckering, then wrinkling, then turning colors: ink blue, white, burgundy. I was losing my ability to steer the scooter, but I was hoping that Isabel wouldn't notice. The asphalt road underneath the tires was turning to oil. I was certain we would sink any minute.

My head was chiming. I could hear the swish of blood behind my ears.

Isabel tapped me on the shoulder and pointed up ahead to a slice of gravel road that led into the trees. She spoke. Her words came out too slow.

I maneuvered the scooter to the left. Even in the middle of the day, it was dark under the canopy of trees; only bits of sky burned through the gaps between the leaves high above our heads. It was quiet, but not quiet. Of course, there was the constant sputtering of the scooter's engine, but in addition to that, I could hear the movement of things large and small scampering through the underbrush and leaping from limb to limb. Those large and small things had sharp eyes that watched us with distrust and wondered who we were to come this way.

The gravel road eventually narrowed until it was little more than a dirt path not three feet wide.

The air in the forest was thick, made thicker by the mosquitoes. I swished the saliva in my mouth then swallowed. It tasted wrong, like rust.

Dry as a bone. Mad as a hatter.

The scenery wasn't changing: I was. Isabel had been too close for too long.

"I need to stop," I said. My voice boomed against my eardrums.

"We're almost there!" Isabel threw one arm out from under the blanket to point into a gap in the trees up ahead, and her thumbnail grazed my cheek. It felt like a razor blade. I had to bite the inside of my mouth to keep from crying out.

"There's a field up ahead." Her breath hit my ear. It burned. "There should be a cabin just on the far side of it."

I narrowed my eyes and saw only a shimmering expanse of green. I'd remembered something like this happening before, when I'd fallen into Isabel's courtyard. The plants were breathing. I could hear them, taking in a collective, sucking breath and letting out a huge, hot sigh. Icy beads of sweat trickled down my face from my hairline to my jaw. The trails they left sizzled against my skin.

Hot as a hare.

I couldn't steer anymore. I mumbled an apology as the scooter veered to the side into the high grass, where it almost immediately ground to halt. Isabel's hands were around my waist, pulling me away from the falling scooter by my belt loops. Together we tumbled into the mud. I landed faceup, staring at a blazing yellow sky. Isabel's arms were around me again. She was trying to turn me over and position me onto my hands and knees.

"Put your finger down your throat!" she demanded.

I did as I was told, placing the tip of my pointer finger against the very back crest of my tongue. My stomach heaved violently, but nothing came out. In my blurry peripheral vision, I could see the white corners of Isabel's blanket. They were fluttering. The trees continued to breathe: in, out, in, out.

Some . . . *thing* appeared in front of my face. I blinked. That didn't help.

Blind as a bat.

"It's water," I heard Isabel say. "Drink."

With trembling, mud-caked fingers, I gently took the bottle as if it was a newborn creature. I drank and immediately spit. The water tasted bitter and thick. Isabel cursed in Spanish.

"Lucas, can you stand?"

Before waiting for an answer, she wrapped her arms around my waist from behind and hauled me to my feet.

"I can see the cabin," she shouted. "It's just a little ways up. Walk. *Walk!*"

The command made sense, but I had no idea how to put it into action. Isabel latched on to the folds of my jeans and started tugging. Oh, yeah: *walk.*

I took a couple of awkward steps before turning my face to hers. What looked like small white bugs were walking down her cheeks, leaving nearly invisible trails of ooze on her hair and skin.

No. Not bugs, stupid. Rain. It was raining. It was always raining.

"You saved me," I muttered. It was a dumb, drunk thing to say, and Isabel knew it.

"Just walk, Lucas," she groaned. "At least try." Then, under her breath, "Let's hope the snakes leave you alone."

The fact that she didn't say "us" didn't escape my addled brain. The snakes—like the mosquitoes—had better instincts than to take a bite out of her.

I was aware of the cool drops that were falling on me from above, but still, I was burning up. Sweat poured down my neck and leaked from my armpits down the sides of my torso. My mouth felt like it was stuffed with wadded-up pieces of paper and glue. When my eyes were open I saw only piercing white light and the surreal, pulsing leaves of grass, so I walked with them closed, letting Isabel guide me.

It was a struggle to just drag one foot in front of the other. My head throbbed and my skin was on fire. The feeling in my stomach had moved past nausea to searing pain that was trickling down my arms and into my fingers. The rain, as it fell on my face and my shoulders, felt like thousands of tiny pinpricks.

I thought of Celia, and was so pissed at myself I nearly fell to my knees. I'd never get to her because I was going to die out in some godforsaken field in the middle of Puerto Rico.

"Stop," I slurred, opening my eyes to slits and smacking my dried-out lips together. "Isabel, stop for a second."

She did as I asked, turning to put one hand on my chest to steady me. "What?" she demanded.

I swallowed, furrowed my brow, and focused on forming words that made perfect sense in that delirious moment: "I want you to kiss me."

For several seconds, Isabel stared at me in silence. Then she yanked on my jacket to get me moving forward again.

"Shut up, Lucas. Just keep walking."

"Please," I implored. "I want you to. Your mouth . . . it reminds me of . . . "

Isabel shoved me forward, hard. The side of my body collided with a rough surface, and I slid to the ground, my legs now completely useless. The right side of my face landed in a puddle of cool, muddy water. The fingers of my right hand crept across the ground for something to latch on to and found a hunk of old wood.

Isabel crouched down directly in front of me, but I could barely make out her face. With the bright sun at her back, she was all shadows and black hair. Her blanket must've fallen from her shoulders.

"You're sick," she snarled. "You always say stupid things to me while you're sick."

Isabel disappeared. I lay there, the muddy water splashing gently against my cheek. My hand clung to the slick, wet chunk of wood. I took comfort in touching something solid.

When Isabel came back, she knelt down and told me we were alone, that her dad must have taken the girls to the other cabin. She said something else, but her words were starting to sound more and more distant. I closed my eyes. They were sore and tired. I needed just a moment to rest them.

I passed out, and of course, I dreamed. I dreamed of Rico and Carlos and me swimming at Condado Beach. I was out in the water, far away from my friends, floating on my back. Something bumped my shoulder. I looked over and saw a foot wrapped in leaves. Something bumped my knee. It was an arm, bloated and shark-bit. Fingers under the dark water started pawing at my back. Hands broke the surface, grabbing at my arms and legs and trying to pull me under. Ragged fingernails tore at my skin. I opened my mouth to scream, only to have the black water fill my lungs. I sank. Down, down.

The dream changed. I found myself standing on the shore of an unfamiliar beach, in the stark light of day, watching an old man and his three-legged dog emerge from the tree line and limp toward me. When they were close, the old man finally spoke. He said that strange and uncertain gods once roamed this beach, but they had decided not to come here anymore. They'd been waiting for the return of their bohique, he said, but they got tired. The spirits of the people, though, they're still around, but they're almost deaf from not being spoken to for so long. The old man leaned in and smiled a toothless smile. His breath smelled sweet, too sweet, like red licorice.

He told me that I'd have to yell very loud to get the gods' attention, but even then they might ignore me if I insisted on speaking to them in my brittle, ugly language.

Eventually, the man and his dog hobbled away, and I turned to face a rough sea and a sky in which a storm was swirling.

TWENTY-TWO

MY EYES FLEW open. Someone was pounding on the walls so hard that the floor underneath me was shaking. There was a shrieking sound, familiar yet terrifying.

The pounding stopped. I thought I might've still been dreaming until I drew a slow breath, and the bitter stench of dried sweat filled my nose—not the stuff of dreams. I pushed myself to seated and noticed by the dim light that I was caked in mud: my fingers, my hands, my knees. My once-black canvas shoes were now two crusty, indistinct masses.

Again, that shriek. The walls rumbled. The wind pushed itself through tiny cracks. I looked up and saw a lit oil lantern, the metal kind someone would have taken camping fifty years ago, rattling on a rickety table behind my head.

"You're up." Isabel's voice came from several feet away. She was sitting in front of a darkened window with her back toward me, her now-filthy blanket of leaves draped loosely around her shoulders.

She winced, pressing her right hand against her ear as if to protect it from a loud, sharp noise. I couldn't hear anything except the persistent sounds of rain and wind.

I glanced at my watch, but the face was cracked. The time had stopped just after two in the afternoon.

"How long was I out?"

"Not long," Isabel replied. "A couple of hours."

"Better than three days." I dragged a cold, mud-caked palm across my forehead. "That must mean I'm becoming immune to you."

She laughed, and I wished she hadn't. It sounded terrible, phlegmatic and low. "I seriously doubt that. I think it has more to do with the fact that you didn't put your lips on me this time. Despite your persistence. And the extra layer of that jacket might have helped."

I frowned, confused. Memories, dreams, and stories were all colliding and melting together in my head. "Did I . . . ?"

The wind was a constant whistle that was high, urgent, and horrifying. I shivered even though I wasn't cold, and the hairs on my arms stood on end. I felt like I was surrounded by something huge and determined to tear me apart.

My head burst with pain. I pressed the heel of my hand against my forehead. "We have to keep going." I swallowed. My mouth was dry and tasted like metal. "Just give me a minute."

"I told you there would be a storm."

"Your hurricane goddess is mad again." I leaned against

the wall behind me and extended my rigid legs, grimacing as my knee and ankle joints popped.

Isabel was gazing out the window in front of her, but for what, I had no idea. The entire pane of glass was obscured by a sheet of falling water. "You don't believe in her," she said.

"Of course I do." Of course I did.

She sighed. "You aren't like my dad. It took him so long to believe. When my mom told him about being cursed by her brother, he didn't believe her. He told me that while she was pregnant, she kept insisting that, instead of a baby inside her, there was a monster, turning and twisting in poison. When she dreamed at night, she could see its green skin. She would die, she was certain, when she gave birth because the poison inside her belly would seep out and seize her heart. She was convinced that I would live and carry her curse, but that I would only survive if I was surrounded by poison, like I'd been inside her. My dad had always kept some of his specimens in the courtyard, but my mom begged him to go out into the forests and find more. She wanted him to fill the courtyard with plants, and she cried when he wouldn't do it."

As Isabel spoke, I searched for my pulse. When my fingers found it, it seemed to be vibrating rather than pulsing. "That's why he started keeping all the plants?"

"No," Isabel scoffed. "He told her that he thought she was marvelous, one of a kind, but he didn't believe her stories about gods and curses. My dad said I refused to nurse for days. My mom went silent and would sit there, blank-faced and motionless, as I wailed for food. My dad would try to take me from her arms, but my mom would only scream and hold me tight against her. Or she'd threaten him, dare him to step closer, say that if he did, she'd toss me over the courtyard wall and into the ocean. Days passed before my dad ran across town to find formula. When he came back, my mother was gone. I was alone, on the floor, asleep, wrapped in a blanket stuffed with cup of gold and sucking quietly on a columbine flower. I wish she'd taken me with her, wherever she went."

"Why didn't he take you to a hospital?"

Isabel gave me a pitying glance. "Because I wasn't sick."

"How many girls have there been, Isabel? You have to have an idea."

"Maybe ten," she said. "All in the last couple of years."

Ten girls, all gone to the water—all of them, for the most part, forgotten. Until Sara, the girl from Florida, the non-island girl.

"Who are they?" I asked. "What are their names?"

"I don't know." Isabel paused, gazing into the corner of the room. "I search my dad's bags and files to find things. Of theirs. Scraps of paper from pockets: receipts, to-do lists, gum wrappers. Bobby pins, barrettes, rings made from cheap silver with plastic stones. I keep them—like I keep the wishes. I used to make up stories about these girls based on the scraps they left behind, but I don't anymore."

"Why?"

Isabel let the question hang, like she was ashamed and wanted me to learn from my mistake of asking it.

How strong was the fabric of a story?

If it was well made, it was stronger than a human body. It could hold up for years and years, never fraying, never growing stiff.

To me, stories were stronger than the truth. Maybe this is what had led to my belief in heroes—that I could *be* the hero—and in worthy, but imperfect villains.

Of course, Isabel thought differently. To her, the girls—their bodies and the artifacts they left behind—were truer and stronger than whatever story could be spun about them.

I glanced over my shoulder to a set of ancient bed frames. The mattresses to both were missing and the wrought iron frames were rusted—like Isabel's voice—as if they'd been left out in the rain and open salty air for months.

That reminded me: the scooter.

"I need to move the . . . "

"I moved it," Isabel said quickly, not turning to look in my direction. "There's a small shed out back. There are gaps in the roof, but it's the best that I could do. It'll be fine."

She held up the note the old woman had given her and waved it in the air.

"It's a burden, you know, being the vessel for everyone's wishes. I want to help them. But of course I can't."

At last, she turned away from the window. When I saw her face, I snatched the lantern off the table behind me and held it up between us. The color of her skin was a sickly, almost pale shade of gray-green and it seemed barely able to stretch over her cheekbones. Her lips were white and blistered at the corners. A bruise ran down the length of her throat. I caught a glimpse of the leaves that made up the blanket's underside; they were withering, their edges brown and brittle.

"I don't know how much longer." She swallowed and looked down to the bruises covering the backs of her hands. "The storm probably won't break in time."

"How long was I out?"

Isabel pressed her cracked lips together. Another wave of wind crashed into the walls, causing the rotten wood and the rusty nails that held the cabin together to shudder and groan.

"*Isabel*. How long was I out?"

She looked away. "A few hours—four maybe. Possibly more."

I scrambled to my feet and threw a hand against the wall for balance.

"Why are you even still here? Why didn't you just leave while I was passed out and finish this yourself?"

One of Isabel's hands was resting on the floor next to her. I watched as her fingernails dug into the old wood as she spoke. "The weather got worse. I couldn't just leave you."

"You're dying! You need to be anywhere *but* here— out looking for plants or on your way back home to your courtyard."

Isabel dove toward me and flung a dirt-covered finger in my face. Her eyes, ringed with deep, near-black purple, gleamed with anger.

"I thought you understood!" she seethed. "I'm not going back to that house. I can't live there anymore. *This* is my fate. You've heard the stories about when the Taíno finally realized they were about to be forced onto sugar plantations and lose the freedom they'd always known, the bravest ones came out here and hanged themselves in the trees."

I'd heard those stories, yeah. The señoras had told them to me when I was a boy.

Isabel stood and pressed her palm against the window-pane. Her chest rose and fell at an erratic pace. "They refused to be slaves. Their spirits are still here protecting the island, and I am one of them. My home is out here. If the storm breaks we'll still go after Celia and the other girl—Lina—but you have to promise me that when this is all done you won't take me back to San Juan."

I was reeling and nauseous. It was too much to consider: saving the girls while allowing Isabel to die. It was clear, however, that's exactly the scenario she had in mind since the moment her father hit the floor—maybe even since before then.

"If it comes down to me or the girls," she continued, "you have to choose them. *I* choose them. They deserve it. I don't. I don't want to live my life in that prison anymore."

Isabel—the determined, bull-headed combatant—glared

at me, daring me to defy her. If there was one thing I'd learned from this version of her, it was that outright defiance did not work.

So I lied, with a cringe to make it seem convincing: "I promise I won't take you back."

She nodded, evidently satisfied.

After depleting what little strength she had, Isabel teetered, checked her balance, and collapsed clumsily against the wall. She flipped a long wet strand of hair over her shoulder, covered her head with her blanket, and closed her eyes. She was quiet for a long time.

"She wanted you to stay." Isabel yanked hard on one of the leaves, separating it entirely from the blanket. A wisp of curled black thread hung from it.

"What are you talking about?"

"You, Lucas, were Marisol's wish," Isabel said. "She wished you would stay on the island so that the two of you could be together."

"Oh *God*, Isabel," I groaned, raking my mud-flecked fingers through my mud-flecked hair. "What are you doing to me?"

The answer was easy: She was killing me. With poison. From heartbreak.

"I'm sorry," Isabel whispered.

If Isabel had anything left to say, her words would have been drowned out by the wind, which screamed with a fury that pulled the air from my stomach. I watched as the front door trembled, then shook with determination against its weak hinges and rusty lock. The storm wasn't content being outside anymore. It wanted in. After just seconds of fighting, the lock gave up. The door was ripped from its frame and swung inward, attached to the house now only by its lower hinge. The wind howled again. It filled the room, filled *me*. I pressed my palms against my ears, but the roar seeped between my fingers and into my skin.

The only thing I could think to do was scream right back and try to convince the storm that I wasn't scared. Then I turned to Isabel. Her hair and blanket rippled around her body. She was glaring out the door, into the swallowing darkness. She was furious.

The bed behind me squealed as its legs were dragged across the floor. Next to my head, the oil lamp, as if picked up by a shaky, invisible hand, rattled across the surface of its table, hovered on the edge, and then crashed to the ground. In an instant, its once-tiny flame spread into a sheet across the floor.

TWENTY-THREE

THE FIRE CAUGHT Isabel's blanket, singeing its edges and causing a toxic stink. Instead of beating out the flames, Isabel gazed warily at the smoldering fabric the way someone might gaze upon an unwelcome person standing in her doorway.

When it became clear Isabel wasn't moving, I slung my arms around her waist and lifted her near-weightless body. Pain spiked in my head. I threw out my left hand to brace myself against the wall, and something large and sharp, the exposed end of an old nail, punctured my palm. Fresh blood burst from my skin.

The front door was swinging madly on its remaining hinge. I grabbed it with my bloody hand to keep it steady and carried Isabel into the merciless rain. Outside, the winds came from every direction, causing the tall grass and Isabel's hair to whip and twirl. Isabel started yelling in Spanish, even though her voice was no match for sounds of the storm.

I placed her down on her feet. She swayed slightly but then regained her balance.

"Wait here!" I shouted.

My mission was to find the scooter, but the smoke and rain and flakes of ash from the cabin made that mission hard. Staying upright, let alone moving forward, was nearly impossible. My legs almost immediately fatigued as I trudged through shin-deep pools of water and muck. I was dizzy and thirsty. Nearby, the cabin pulsed with a wet heat.

A gust of wind plowed into me from behind, spun me one hundred and eighty degrees, and threw me onto my knees. I sucked rainwater off the ground and was reminded of my insignificance.

I hauled myself to standing, turned, and fought the wall of wind until I finally found the shed. The door was missing, and I could see the scooter leaning against a metal table on which rusty tools had been carelessly left and were now rattling as if they were alive and angry about it. Isabel was right about the roof. The rain poured freely through gaps created by missing or rotted boards.

I dragged the scooter out of the shed and back into the field, climbed on, and twisted the key in the ignition. It didn't catch. I counted off five seconds and tried again. Nothing.

I offered a desperate prayer to the goddess who makes the storms. I couldn't remember her name and hoped she wouldn't mind. I told her I was sorry that she was angry. I was sorry for men like my father and Dr. Ford, men who come to the island only to tear things down, build things that don't belong, and make girls disappear. Maybe she was upset with me. I was no saint. I'd done some shitty things in my life, but I was trying to do better.

"Would you please give me a break?" I cried out.

I twisted the key in the ignition again. It caught, and I cried out in triumph. Clicking on the single headlight, I released the hand brake and lunged forward, the wheels of the tires spitting up mud and grass behind me.

Isabel was where I'd left her, standing in the field and struggling to keep the blanket around her shoulders while the wind fought to claim it. When she saw me coming, she wiped the hair out of her face and motioned to the cabin, which had started to sway. The nails and windowpanes squealed loudly against the strain of the heat and expanding wood.

The wind won, as it does, ripping Isabel's blanket of leaves from her hands and carrying it high in the sky. Isabel held her arms up, her fingers splayed desperately.

"Forget it!" I yelled. "Just get on!"

I slowed down enough for her to climb onto the scooter, and together we burst through the field. Just before we entered the dense mass of trees, I turned to look over my shoulder and saw the cabin lift from its foundation. For a long second, the fragile structure seemed to hover, perfectly intact, no more than a foot off the ground. Then it crashed down into a heap of splintered wood and rusted metal. The wind screamed its victory.

Isabel wailed and buried her head between my shoulder blades. I turned to refocus my efforts on getting us through the forest in one piece. It seemed unlikely. Above our heads, the rain hit the wide leaves of the palms and then poured down onto our heads in thick streams. Beneath us, the ground was more uneven than it had been out in the field. The path we'd been on a few hours ago had turned to sludge. The wind hurled palm fronds into the side of my face. They stung like slaps.

"Where do we go?" I shouted back over my shoulder.

"Back to the main road! Then left toward Rincón."

What should've taken minutes seemed to last hours. If the goddess had somehow magically started Rico's scooter, she must have dusted off her hands and decided that was enough for the day.

All I saw were trees and mud and water. The single headlight didn't illuminate shit. Every time the front tire caught a root or a rock, my entire body tensed in anticipation of a blowout. I tried not to think about missing a turn and wrapping us around the trunk of a tree. I imagined someone years from now finding our sun-bleached skeletons alongside the rusted and mangled carcass of a scooter. The stories people would tell about us would pale in comparison to the truth. What a sad thing it would be to simply disappear in this forest.

The mud road beneath the scooter's tires eventually

changed to a gravelly slush, and then, once we finally turned onto the main highway, to slick asphalt.

The rain still poured down from the gunmetal clouds that swirled and cracked, and there was paltry traction between Rico's balding tires and the wet road. We drove with the current, with the rain rushing along with us back to its source: that sea into which I'd always wanted to disappear. But not today.

I gripped the handlebars, bracing for the hissing winds that seemed bent on sending us spiraling into the sky. My ears were ringing, probably because I was clamping my jaw shut with such force that I was surprised my teeth didn't shatter. More than once I had to remind myself to exhale after anxiously holding my breath until my vision had started to blur.

But neither the unrelenting weather nor the awful conditions of the road distracted me from the fact that Isabel, without the protection of her leaves, was fading fast. Her body felt like a wet sack flung against my back.

All I could do was keep driving. The landscape tore by, dark and frenzied.

A few miles down the road we sped past a reflective sign announcing we'd arrived in Isabela, a town originally named for the queen of Spain, now known for its beaches and cockfights. As we passed the dark town, only a few lights twinkled from buildings far off in the distance. Like San Juan, Isabela was another sea-facing city where people were used to sealing themselves into their homes to wait patiently for the world to find its balance again. They knew the score. Storms come; storms go.

For a long time the road was empty, except for our little scooter, the rain coming down in sheets, the angry wind, and the spinning gray clouds. Eventually, we passed another sign, this one for the town of Aguadilla, and I felt Isabel shift behind me. She tugged on my jacket with her thin fingers, trying to pull us closer. I leaned back, burning and shivering as her wet lips grazed my ear. She swallowed and took a couple of breaths in preparation to speak.

"Turn . . . here." There was an extended pause between the two words. "To the right."

I did as she asked, maneuvering the scooter onto a barely visible road that led into a thicket of trees.

I let out the throttle and shot forward. With the thin stretch of road in front of us bubbling like furiously boiling water, there was no way I could've seen the spikes.

TWENTY-FOUR

THE TIRES BLEW out in two loud, successive pops, causing the scooter to shake violently as if suddenly possessed. Despite my best efforts to keep a hold of the handlebars, I flew into the air and landed face-first in the mud. I heard a sharp crack as my right wrist twisted under my body at an unnatural angle. I cried out, my mouth filling with brackish water, as I started to float and move along with the current. With my good hand, I made a fist and slammed it through the water and into the mud to keep from being washed away.

I crawled to my knees and took several gasping breaths as I tested the mobility of each of the fingers of my right hand. Thin ribbons of pain shot all the way up into my jaw.

Despite that, I managed to stand, disoriented, in a wide-leg stance. In the middle of the road a few yards back, the scooter was on its side, crushed. Though its front and back tires were pulverized down to the rims, the motor was still despondently firing. What a champ.

A few feet beyond the scooter, a piece of metal stuck up from the ground, then another right next to it, then another.

I looked down the road in the opposite direction but couldn't see anything aside from rain and trees.

"Isabel!"

A thin, pale hand shot up from the other side of the road. Cradling my lame arm, I trudged forward. Isabel was crouching in the underbrush near the trunk of a massive tree. As I approached, she stood abruptly.

"Watch it!"

Her arm was outstretched, and around her wrist were two thick leaves, secured in knots. Others were shoved under the straps of her tank top, close to her heart. Despite a line of shallow cuts running across her cheek, Isabel was, of all things, smiling. It was a wan smile on a tired face, but a smile nonetheless. She held up her other wrist, around which were the same leaves tied in the same way.

"Dumb cane!" she exclaimed.

"So, you'll be all right?" I asked.

Isabel stepped out of the underbrush and into the road. "For now. How about you?"

"I'm okay." In an attempt to mask the pain, I bit down on the inside of my lip. "Our ride's wrecked, though."

Isabel's eyes shifted to the remains of Rico's scooter, then to the road ahead.

"So we run," she said.

So we ran, or at least tried to run, down a road turned to river in the driving rain. I kept my wrist close to my body, because when I let it swing down by my side the pain was unbearable.

Eventually, we turned a corner. Up ahead was the glow of a faint light. The sight of it caused both of us to run faster, kicking up the thick mud and water under our feet.

Soon, what had been just a small light took the shape of a white, luminescent square: a window. Something moved across it. While it could've been a palm frond or a coconut falling from one of the trees, I was hoping it was a girl.

The cabin that eventually came into focus was bigger than the one we'd just seen lifted up into the sky and then thrown to the ground. It was sturdier, cobbled together out of large, round stones and bolstered by wooden beams. Rather than standing unprotected in the middle of a field and exposed to the elements, this one was nestled in a kind of alcove, surrounded on three sides by dense trees.

In the road, maybe forty yards in front of the house, was a light blue Mercedes-Benz, the old kind with the hubcaps that boasted the Mercedes symbol and matched the car's color. As we neared it, Isabel slowed to a stop, taking in the house, the trees, the car.

"He must've passed us while we were back at the other cabin. I don't think the police are coming this way, or else he wouldn't have put down the spikes. Those were just for us."

"Maybe, but Mara Lopez tracked me down at some random church in the dead of night, so I doubt a rainstorm and some spikes are going to stop her."

Isabel dug into her back pocket and held out the damp and mud-splattered note that the woman from Mayagüez had given her.

"Take this," she said.

"Why? What am I supposed to do with it?"

"Put it with the others. That's all I did. People need something to put their hope in." Isabel swallowed and nodded her head as if convincing herself that she was doing the right thing. Stepping forward, she shoved the note into the front pocket of my jeans. "You be the wishing fountain now."

Without waiting for a reply, Isabel took off toward the house. As she neared one of the front windows, she crouched to peer through it. I took my place beside her. The inside of the house was dark, except for a couple of lanterns burning on small bedside tables. Through the muted light all I could make out were the faint outlines of two beds, much like those in the other cabin, and across the room from those, a long table about the height of a kitchen counter. Everything else was fogged up, dark, and indistinct.

"Lucas," Isabel hissed. "*Mira*. Look!" She pointed at the front door. A padlock the size of my fist hung from the handle. Isabel gave it a tug. "He's nearby or else he would've taken his car."

"I'll go around the side," I said, "and see if I can find something we can use to smash the lock."

I scanned the dark ground around the perimeter of the house. The rain rolled off the roof and steadily dripped from the eaves onto my shoulder. The runoff found a rhythm. It hit harder—more urgently. Then, a blast of cold hit the back of my neck.

I spun around and saw the girl; she was at least six feet away, partially hidden in the shadows of the trees. Her feet were bare and covered in sand; her skin was concrete-gray. She was wearing a pale, apple-green sundress. Its hem fell to her ankles. The wind continued to swirl, but the fabric of her dress didn't rustle; the ends of her hair weren't picked up and tossed around. She was soaked even though the rain seemed to bend and part around her.

She wasn't Marisol. She wasn't Sara.

"Water." Her voice was a chorus. "He's by the water."

The girl took a single step forward, toward me, away from the trees. Isabel called out my name, and my head whipped toward the sound. I felt the disappeared girl come close. Her breath was cold and smelled like cinnamon. I would ask her questions: *What's your name? Who misses you?* But when I turned back toward her, there were several feet between us again.

She opened her mouth. Isabel's voice came from it: "Lucas!"

I took a stagger-step forward before turning and running to the front of the house, where Isabel was attacking the door with a large, jagged rock. She struck the lock once, twice, and on the third time it broke from the wood frame. The wind caught the door, and it immediately swung inward, spraying rainwater into the dark room. Pieces of paper scattered, and small, unidentifiable objects skittered across the floor. Something large and solid tipped onto its side and rolled across a hard surface. For a split second, it was still. Then: the firecracker-pop of glass breaking.

Isabel and I tumbled inside, and I pushed the door closed behind us. Because of the broken lock, I had to stand with my back against the wood. In the relative quiet, a brew of smells hit my nose: ammonia, bleach, dried sweat on unwashed skin, the unmistakably sweet stench of rot.

"We're too late," Isabel declared.

I nearly conceded, but then the sound of fabric rustling came from one of the beds, followed by the gasp of a child startled out of sleep.

"Hello?" I called out.

I dragged a squat table in front of the door to hold it in place. Grabbing a lit lantern from the ground, I held it up to the closest of the twin beds. The head of a small dark-haired girl emerged from underneath the covers.

"Celia?"

I rushed forward, but Isabel smacked her palm against my chest. "Don't touch her!" She dropped her hand and leaned in. "You don't know what she's like anymore."

What she's *like*: near death, full of poison, a small and fragile monster. Just like Isabel.

I approached Celia, scanning her face and what I could see of her arms for red rashes or white blisters, but there was no sign of her being sick or hurt. Leaves weren't shoved under her bedcovers, pressed against her skin, or threaded through her hair.

I let out a yelp of victory. I couldn't help it. I'd done it. I'd beaten the police and a mad scientist and a curse and a storm and a goddess who makes storms, and here Celia was, alive and seemingly well, right in front of me. It was so brilliant.

I crouched down at Celia's bedside, and Isabel appeared over my shoulder, holding another lantern.

"You remember me, right?" I asked.

Celia nodded.

"Are you okay?"

Celia's eyes sparked with amusement as she watched the water drip from my clothes onto her bed. "You're wet."

I smiled. "Yeah, I know. We got caught in the rain. Here." I pulled the wolf charm from my pocket and placed it in her hand. "You lost this."

"Where'd you find it?"

"She found it," I said, motioning over my shoulder to Isabel. "So you feel all right? Are you sure? No stomachache? No itchy skin?"

Celia shook her head.

"You really think she's fine?" Isabel asked.

"She seems like it."

"Still . . . We should get her out of here. Quickly."

Isabel went off to inspect the rest of the room. First, she leaned over the unmade bed next to Celia's, running her hand over the mattress. Past the beds, a crude divider made from an old sheet was hanging from hooks in the ceiling. Isabel pulled it back, revealing a cot with a neatly folded blanket placed across its end. An overturned crate served as a makeshift nightstand, and books and journals were stacked at least two feet high on it. Fastened to the wall over the cot was a rough-hewn shelf filled with more books, along with what looked like a wooden cigar box and a photo in a frame. Isabel picked up the photo and looked it over, her eyes revealing nothing.

"What's wrong with your hand?" Celia asked me. "Did you hurt it? If you hurt it, the doctor will make it better for you."

"Who else is here, Celia?" Isabel asked from across the room, slamming down the picture frame. She knelt down next to her dad's cot, flicked a small plastic cigarette lighter that she'd found, and lit yet another lantern that was sitting atop a couple of hardback books. "Is there a girl named Lina?"

"Lina was here, but not for very long," Celia replied. "She was sick. The doctor said she might have to go to the hospital. I heard him come and take her out of bed."

"How long ago was that?" I asked.

Celia shrugged and picked at the loose threads on the edge of her blanket. "I don't know. It was during the storm. Are you a saint?" she asked suddenly, turning her head toward Isabel. "You look like a saint from the pictures in church."

I glanced at Isabel. The shadows in the cabin hid the sickly color of her skin, and her face glowed in the lanternlight.

"I'm not a saint." Isabel stepped over to a long wooden table in the middle of the room. An array of leaves in various stages of decomposition and more stacks of books and paper covered it. There was also a set of eyeglasses, a pair of thick gloves, a surgical mask, and a collection of pencils, most of them worn down to nubs. Isabel picked up one of the books at random, a thick, hardcover volume, and started flipping through its pages.

"I'm the doctor's daughter," she said.

"Are you magical?" Celia asked, her eyes widening. "Your dad tells stories about you. He says you're magic."

Isabel shut the book and glared at the little girl. The corner of her mouth twitched.

"Take the girl," Isabel demanded, grabbing a set of keys from the table and tossing them to me. "Now. Use his car. Go back to Arecibo and get her to a doctor. Be sure to keep her wrapped her in a blanket—just in case—and say she's possibly been exposed to poisonous plants. Do something about your wrist as well. It looks terrible."

I stood. "What about you?"

Isabel didn't answer. Instead, she grabbed the two lanterns she'd recently lit, went over to the door, and set them down by her feet. Using her teeth, she tore the leaves from her wrists and then yanked the others out from under her shirt. A gust of wind blew open the door, knocking back the table, and throwing Isabel slightly off balance. The lanterns almost tipped over, but Isabel grabbed them just in time.

"What about you?" I repeated, rushing toward her. "We still have to find Lina."

"Wake up, Lucas!" Isabel hissed. "Lina's dead. My dad took her out to the beach to dump her body, and that's where I'm going."

Water, the girl had said. *He's by the water.*

"Just wait a minute." My voice was trembling. "We have your dad's car. It'll take a couple of hours to get back to San Juan. We'll drop off Celia. After that we'll find more plants and worry about your dad from there."

"I told you I'm not going back," Isabel said. "I thought you understood."

"Isabel." I lifted my good hand to hold hers. She dodged away.

"You promised me, Lucas! Save the girl."

"Isabel, you can't just leave!" I reached for the soaked fabric of her shirt, but she dodged me again and knelt down to pick up one of the lanterns. She rested her fingertips on one of my muddy shoes. Her gesture was so careful, like that of a tentative ghost.

Isabel stood, holding a lantern in each of her hands. She stepped to the side to peer once more into the small cabin. Then, finally, her eyes met mine. They were full of fire and fight.

"I would watch you when you would stand by the water," she said. "The way you looked out to the horizon . . . I knew we were the same. We both wanted something. We weren't really sure what it was, or if we deserved it . . . But now we know, and now we have it."

"Isabel. What are you doing?"

"My life . . . " she began. "This is not a life. I'm sorry, Lucas."

"Isabel . . ."

She smiled, just a little. "You are the only one to have your wish come true."

"Isabel!" I shrieked.

She wouldn't hear me out. Instead, she took a step back and hurled one of the lanterns at the cabin's back wall, where it burst into flames.

TWENTY-FIVE

CELIA STARTED SCREAMING. Red-orange flames clawed the walls, and near-white flecks of ash drifted in front of my face and landed on my hands. *Moths*, I thought. *They look like moths.* Dry wood and paper crackled and turned black. Windowpanes groaned from the extreme heat and pressure until, finally, they shattered. Glowing embers hit the beds and singed the blankets. Smoke rose and rolled across the beams of the ceiling. The oil lantern next to Celia's bed exploded, causing the little girl to toss off her covers and run toward me. She clung to my legs and let out another ear-splitting wail. She clung tight, burying her face into wet denim.

Isabel was gone, disappeared.

I scooped up Celia with my good arm and carried her out into the relentless rain.

I was grateful for the warm, fat drops that fell on my face as I slogged through the mud toward Dr. Ford's Mercedes.

They were soothing and helped to wash the sting from my eyes. When we reached the car, I put Celia down. Her bare feet sank several inches into the spongy earth.

I fumbled with the unfamiliar keys for a few seconds before managing to unlock the back door. I held it open, but the girl didn't move. I shouted her name, but she just stood there, as if having been absorbed by the ground, staring in silent horror at the cabin.

"Get in the car!"

Still nothing.

It was only after I'd lifted her up and placed her into the backseat that I realized I hadn't wrapped her in a blanket. Amid the chaos of the fire, it had slipped my mind.

I recoiled, holding my arms up to my eyes to search my skin for blisters.

Celia chose to break her silence with a question I couldn't begin to answer: "What's wrong?"

I braced my good hand against the doorframe, bowed my head, and waited for the wave of nausea to come. It didn't. Celia touched my arm and repeated her question.

"Lucas? What's wrong?"

I stared at her small hand against my skin.

"The plants don't make you sick?" I asked.

Celia shook her head. "I don't get sick."

"What about when you touched the doctor? Did he get sick?"

"No." She dropped her hand into her lap. "Why would he?"

"Wait right here!"

I slammed the door shut, and went back to the burning cabin. Even before I reached the door, I could see that most of the interior was engulfed in flames. The scattered pages of Dr. Ford's books were curling and crisp around the edges, and the air was almost completely full of ash and burning paper. Behind the smell of smoke was the bitter stench of leaves releasing their poison.

Covering my nose and mouth with Rico's jacket, I plowed into the dense smoke in the direction of Dr. Ford's cot at the back of the cabin. I found it when my shins collided with the metal frame.

I gathered up the smoldering blanket, caught sight of the photograph Isabel had looked at earlier, and snatched that, too. Bundling the frame in the folds of the blanket, I swung around toward the door, and stopped.

There was no door. Only a curtain of smoke and fire.

I collected all the blessings, prayers, superstitions, luck, and enchantments I knew, held the wadded-up blanket in front of my face, and charged forward into the hot, smoking void.

A belt of pain whipped against my right shoulder as I burst through the front door, but beyond that I came out mercifully intact. I trudged through the mud and collapsed into the driver's seat of Dr. Ford's Mercedes.

"Is the doctor's daughter coming with us?" Celia asked as

I slammed the door closed and threw the blanket into the passenger seat.

Wiping the smoke-induced tears from my eyes, I pretended to not hear her. Then I craned my head so that I could look at my shoulder. A ragged hole had burned through layers of fabric, revealing an oozing flesh wound. Smoke rose from its edges; it stunk. My stomach kicked with nausea, and I had to turn away. Remembering the photograph, I reached across the seat with my left hand and pulled it from the still-warm folds of the blanket.

The glass of the frame was cracked, either from the heat or from Isabel's having slammed it down. The picture behind the fractured glass, though, was perfectly clear.

I'd assumed that what Isabel had seen on that shelf was a photograph of herself—younger, happier, and without the weight of all the disappeared girls on her shoulders. Instead, the photo had captured a younger version of her dad, next to a beautiful woman with long dark hair who must have been Isabel's mother. They were standing together in the courtyard of their house at the end of Calle Sol. They were surrounded by plants. He was in a brown suit; she was in a white sundress with the slightly bulging midsection of an expectant mother. They were holding each other's hands, and a large gray bird was perched on Dr. Ford's shoulder. Zabana's free hand rested on her belly. While both the Fords were smiling, Isabel's mother's gaze was directed to some point off in the distance, as if at the very last second before the shutter snapped, something had caught her attention.

I'd known little about Dr. Ford's life aside from the sad stories patched together from Isabel and the señoras of San Juan. Those stories all existed in that magical space between truth and fiction, where most of the stories about Puerto Rico existed. That magical space was what the photograph had captured: two people, one happy about his impending child, the other distracted by something from either the past or the future—something there, but not there.

I tossed the frame down and with a single twist of the key, brought the engine of the old car rumbling to life. I clicked on the headlights and the windshield wipers, pulled the column shifter down into reverse, and pressed gently on the gas.

Miraculously, the tires found traction, and the car slowly started going backward. That miracle, however, was short-lived. The car lurched and stopped. I took my foot off the gas and gave myself to the count of ten before pressing down on the accelerator again. While counting, I listened to the rain pelt the roof and tried to ignore the pain that swelled throughout my body. Each raindrop sounded like an individual ball bearing striking a sheet of metal. Together, they sounded like a sky determined to crush us to death.

A single mosquito had found its way into the car with us. I assumed most of its comrades had been kicked off the island by the hurricane. It flew in dizzy circles before landing on my arm. After I slapped it away, it changed course, flying in a series of even dizzier circles toward Celia in the backseat. It approached her arm, backtracked, approached her face, backtracked. Eventually it settled on the seat beside her. It avoided her—the way the mosquitoes all avoided Isabel.

Celia pulled the smoke-tinged blanket around her shoulders. She was shivering.

"You're sick," I said.

She shook her head, and tiny droplets of water sprayed across the interior of the car.

"Just cold."

I didn't know if I believed her. I needed to get her out of here and to a doctor. I checked everything again—that I was in the right gear, that the parking brake was off—before applying slight pressure to the gas pedal. Over the sound of the rain on the roof, I could hear the back wheels spinning as they struggled to find traction.

Again, I eased off. "Not now. Not now." I slammed my eyes shut, opened them, and started counting again. "One... two... three... four... "

The little girl's voice came from over my shoulder: "What's wrong?"

That question.

I clenched the steering wheel in an effort to hide my frustration. The wiper blades skirted across the windshield, revealing the orange glow of the still-burning structure several yards in front of us.

"Five . . . six . . ."

What was wrong? It wasn't that I was worried about us being consumed by the fire. The car was too far away and the rain was too heavy for the blaze to skip across a large swath of muddy ground. Even if the car never started, the rain would eventually stop, and Celia and I could walk together to Isabela and find help.

What was wrong was that Isabel was gone. Isabel's mother was gone. Marisol was gone. Sara Fikes and Lina Gutierrez were gone.

"Seven . . . eight."

I slammed my foot down on the accelerator. The tires spun furiously. I knew it wouldn't do any good, but I kept my weight on the pedal until the inside of the car started to fill up with the stench of burning oil.

I let off the gas and sat back hard in my seat, crying out in pain from my shoulder. I balled my bad hand into a fist and slammed it down on the steering wheel in sharp, successive whacks. When the pain got unbearable, I collapsed forward, pressed my forehead against the steering wheel, and tried to take deep breaths. They were more like gasps: uncontrolled and uncontrollable.

"We'll have to walk," I gasped. "To Isabela."

"We can't leave," Celia replied. "The doctor's daughter will get lost."

"That's what she wants, Celia! She wants us to leave her here."

Celia grew quiet. My eyes flickered up to the rearview mirror. She was at the brink of tears, and I feared beyond anything else the words that were about to come out of her mouth.

Her small lips trembled. "But I dreamed about her."

As if my heart couldn't break any more. "Everyone dreams about her, Celia."

"She told me that she grants wishes. I wished to go home. I think she's an angel."

"She's *not* an angel." The windshield wipers swished back and forth in a futile gesture. "She's just a girl."

"Why did we dream about her then?"

"I don't know," I replied, exasperated. "But I'm not going to just leave you here while I go try to find her."

Celia sat on the edge of her seat, and leaned in to whisper in my ear. "She must be a ciguapa."

I spun around in my seat. "What?"

"My grandmother told me they were drawn to the water, and that their eyes were sad, and that they were the prettiest girls you'd ever see." She paused. "The doctor's daughter is like that."

The magical ciguapas could also be ugly, my mother had said. *They left tracks that faced backward and lured foolish, hopeful men into thinking they would receive a kiss. Then they would suck the breath out of those foolish men's bodies. They could bewitch you with a glance. They were monsters, vengeful and sad.*

"She's just a girl," I lied.

Celia pointed in the direction of the front window. "I bet she went to the beach. I can show you how to get there. The doctor took me there to hunt for shells."

I turned to look at the fingers of my right hand. They were swollen, no doubt broken, and pulsing with pain. I lifted my head and peered up again into the rearview mirror.

"You're sure you can show me the way?"

The little girl nodded.

"Let's go."

TWENTY-SIX

I HELD CELIA tight against my chest and ran through the trees. My feet plunged deep into pockets of mud and wet sand. My ankles buckled. The rain beat against my face. My soaked clothes, Celia, and the drenched cotton blanket I'd wrapped her in were like iron weights across my chest.

A large, high branch from one of the trees gave in to the relentless wind and rain and crashed to the ground not ten feet in front of us. Water splashed across my eyes and lips. Celia shrieked, buried her head into the crook of my neck, and gripped at my clothes. I peered up to where the branch had fallen, half expecting to see bodies of Taínos swaying from the trees. There were none. I listened for the voices of their spirits to tell me that I was lost and to keep back and out of their business. Those voices never came. I wouldn't have listened to them anyway.

We pressed on. Wind ripped through the trees with such force that my molars rattled and the earth shook. It threw me sideways to the ground and Celia out of my arms. I landed on my burned shoulder and screamed, sure that the island was going to crack in half and that I would fall right in.

If that were the case, I, too, like the spirits in the trees, would never leave. I'd merge with the forest. I'd be the rustle in the leaves. I'd be the rain.

Celia climbed back into my arms, wiped my wet hair away from my eyes and some of the grit from my lips. I trembled at her touch and closed my eyes. She pried my eyelids apart, forcing me to look at her mud-speckled face. She was afraid of the water. I'd forgotten that she couldn't swim.

"We can go back!" I shouted.

That wasn't what Celia wanted. She pointed to the left. There, in a break of the trees, was the furious ocean and a dark, menacing sky that appeared to be continually folding in on itself.

I hauled myself to my feet and regained a good grip on Celia. Stumbling a few more yards through the fallen branches and palm fronds, we finally broke through the trees. The line where sea and sky met was nonexistent. Even from where I was standing, a good forty feet from what should have been the water's edge, the surf crashed around my ankles and calves, at times rising nearly to my knees. The ground beneath me shifted and slipped.

Through the rain that cut down from the sky, I saw the white crests of waves beating their way toward me. I scanned the water for the pale limbs or puffed-up clothing of a little girl named Lina, floating all alone because I'd thrown notes and jumped over a wall. But there was no color, nothing out of the ordinary in this out-of-the ordinary scene, just the hungry waves that gathered everything they could take back with them into the ocean.

I knew Lina was gone, lost to those greedy waters.

Celia pointed again, this time to a spot several yards down the beach. Isabel and her dad were standing apart, facing one another, in water that nearly reached their waists. Isabel was holding her father's sleeve. Her mouth was up near his ear, her lips relaying a message. Her wet hair flew around both their heads.

I cried out to Celia to hang on as I began to stomp farther out into the water.

I watched as Dr. Ford lifted his free hand and placed it on the back of his daughter's head in the effort to try to control the fluttering strands of her hair. Isabel dodged away from his touch. As she stumbled back, her head turned. It was obvious from her expression—collapsed, gray like the roaring storm clouds—that my coming after her had broken her heart. But she had to have known that's what I'd do. She'd watched me. She'd known that ever since I was a kid, I'd been drawn to her house—to *her*. I wanted in, desperately. I wanted to make things right, bring light to her shadowed rooms, and pry her loose from the grip of an old curse.

And yet if I tried to save Isabel Ford—pulled her off this beach against her will and then went running through the forest gathering plants for her until I was ranting and covered in blisters—I would merely be one more person who controlled the curve of her life.

Isabel didn't need a hero. She was saving herself, lifting her own curse, atoning for the Saras and the Marisols and the Linas, and all the other nameless disappeared girls.

Still, I took a step forward, toward Isabel, always toward Isabel, but my foot never found the ocean floor. I was under water; Celia was under water, panicked and thrashing.

The tides kicked and spun both of us, but I managed to fight back and break the surface. Gasping, I pulled Celia up by the armpits. Her head flew back and slammed against my chin. The impact stunned me, and Celia again slipped from my arms and fell back under the churning water. I plunged my hands into the chop and found fabric. I pulled and pulled, frenzied and desperate, but it was just the blanket. I'd lost Celia to the water. After all this, I'd let her fall right out of my hands.

Just then: a head broke the surface. Celia's. It was followed by another. Isabel's. Isabel was holding up Celia while her chin rested on top of the little girl's head. Her forever-melancholy eyes closed slowly, opened slowly, with great effort. She wheezed, sucking strands of her hair, both black and chalk white, into her open mouth.

A sob broke from my chest—not just because Isabel was dying, but also because, out here in the great, wide ocean, she was so small. There needed to be more of her. She had the soul of a giant, and no one would ever know.

"Go!" Isabel tossed Celia to me and then turned. She took a gasping breath before half wading, half swimming back to her father.

This time, I did as Isabel commanded. I paddled back far enough to find semisolid footing and was able to lurch back toward the tree line with Celia in my trembling arms.

"I'm sorry," I sputtered. "Celia, I'm sorry. Are you okay?"

Celia wasn't listening. Her eyes were focused on the girl who had saved her.

I turned. Dr. Ford and Isabel were again facing one another. Isabel could hardly stand, her weight shifting on failing legs. Dr. Ford reached for her again, this time for her hand. Again, she dodged away, but instead of merely stumbling, she fell, sideways into the sea. Dr. Ford was quick. He caught his daughter's wrist with both his hands and strained to pull her limp body from the hungry water. His mouth gaped open as he brought her against his chest and held her there. He buried his face into her hair. His shoulders began to shake. His fingers clung desperately to Isabel's unmoving arms.

"See?" Celia released one of her hands from my shoulders. Again, she brushed the wet hair out of my eyes. "The doctor loves her very much."

"He loves her very much," I echoed.

I watched the doctor's strength dissolve. It happened first in his legs. Then his head lolled. But even as they both dropped like stones into the swirling water, the doctor's arms remained around his daughter.

I waited, desperately scanning the surface. Isabel was in there, somewhere. The water was tossing her around as if she were nothing. It was carrying her and her father out into its cold heart.

I thought of how, just a few hours ago, the sun had shone on Isabel's face. She'd smiled her sad smile and told me it had been years since she'd been on a beach. She'd gazed out into the ocean like it was the most beautiful thing she'd ever seen, like it was waiting for her.

I waited, but the ocean never gave Isabel back. Eventually, I picked up Celia and started back through the rain and muck and trees in the direction of the cabin and the car. Celia's hands rested gently on my wet clothes. She was speaking, but it was in that made-up language of hers, the private one, the one she used to talk to her dolls, the one that sounded like water.

STRANGE AND UNCERTAIN GODS

RICO WAS THE only one of my friends to ever ask about Isabel. The others hadn't known she'd existed, so they couldn't have known she was gone.

Five weeks after I'd walked up that forest path to the cabin, watched the embers dwindle, then set off on foot to the nearest town with Celia clinging to my back, what remained of Rupert Ford washed up on a beach near Rincón. The police identified him by a pocket watch that had his name engraved on the back. He was not mourned.

Isabel remained lost to the ocean, as did Lina Gutierrez.

When Detective Mara Lopez knelt in front of Celia, held her hands, and asked her if I was the man who'd taken her, Celia laughed. She told the detective that Dr. Ford had approached her when she was walking down the street searching for her sister. He showed her a trick, how he could make a cat's cradle using a long loop of string. He asked her if she believed in magic. She trusted him when he told her that he knew where to find Marisol.

She remembered very little about what happened after that—just the smell of something sweet followed by waking up in a warm bed in a small cabin. She told Dr. Ford she was lonely and missed her sister. He found Lina for her.

Despite Celia's story, I was arrested and thrown into a Puerto Rican jail. Every day for a week, Mara Lopez sat me down in a windowless room and pounded me with questions about Marisol and Celia.

Do you not think it a strange coincidence that you had a connection to both victims? What exactly is your interest in poisonous plants? Why would Dr. Ford lie about what you said and where you'd gone? How many times have you been to Rincón? How did you know where to find Celia?

I answered those questions the same way each time: Rupert Ford, once he learned of my interest in botany, had given me a book explaining, among other things, the symptoms of poisoning. That book described the same symptoms that the police claimed Sara and Marisol's bodies showed signs of. I went over to ask Dr. Ford about it. He threatened me. I was defending myself when I pushed him. He fell to the ground and hit his head on the tile. I found the directions to a cabin among some papers in his study, borrowed my friend Rico's scooter, and set off on my own, afraid the police wouldn't believe my story.

Mara Lopez wasn't satisfied. No surprise there.

My face was on the news for several days. People I'd never even met before hated me. People I *had* met hated me even more. I was lucky, however, that the people of San Juan hated the man who lived at the house at the end of Calle Sol more than they could ever hate me.

When I was finally released and returned to my room at the St. Lucia, I found Dr. Ford's book on my bed. The dedication had been altered: *To ~~Zabana~~ Lucas. There is nothing in this or any world strong enough to divide us.* This was added underneath: *I'm sorry for what I've done. Thank you for helping me lift the curse from my house.*

That very same day, I jumped over Isabel's wall and stole away with her trunk of wishes. In other trunks I found the scraps of the girls that Isabel had mentioned back in the cabin—a ripped piece of paper showing the last four digits of a telephone number, a blue plastic barrette dotted with rhinestones, a bracelet made of pale woven string, a single stud earring inlayed with fake turquoise. I could imagine Isabel wearing the bracelet, but the earring, no, and the barrette, probably not, unless it was years ago. It would've been no match for her wild hair.

I debated keeping those scraps, but in the end, left them where they were. When Mara Lopez searched the house, she'd find them, study them, make stories out of them, form conclusions based on them, enter them as evidence. I decided, finally, it was time to leave the detecting to the detective.

Also, Isabel wouldn't have wanted me to take them. She'd say that there's no use for mementos of dead girls I never knew. She wouldn't have wanted me to turn those fragments around in my fingers, and make up stories that served no point other than to answer *what if?* with *what if?* with *what if?*

Even without the scraps, I still thought of those girls, their hair wet, their clothes wet, their feet covered in sand, and I wondered what they had wanted to do with their lives before they ended up that way. Maybe they wanted to move to America; maybe they wanted to learn to play an instrument.

Then the letters started. I'd find them slipped under my door when I woke up in the morning or waiting for me at the front desk. They'd ask for help dealing with the loss of a loved one or finding a lost pet bird. I kept them all in a suitcase.

The mosquitoes left the island as they had come: swiftly and without warning. The weather for the rest of the season was mild. Warm days were punctuated by the occasional sun-shower. For now the island was at peace with herself, but the old people all knew that peace has a short memory and comes with a price.

Only when I left the island later that summer did I start to dream of Isabel again—in all her forms. Her face was indistinct; her skin was a pale shade of green, and instead of hair, long green leaves tumbled down from her scalp. Sometimes she was throwing rocks at my face; sometimes she was sitting on her bed in her room of glass. Sometimes she was standing in the sun at Condado Beach. I also dreamed of her standing in my room, her hair up in a bun, looking at me—frowning, chin tilted down slightly—like I'd broken her heart. Those dreams were the worst. They were even worse than the nightmares that jarred me from sleep, the ones in which she was wrapped in leaves, floating in the middle of the ocean, her lifeless eyes gazing up to the sky. Sometimes I just saw her hair, rippling under water. Sometimes I wondered if it was Isabel I was dreaming or if it was Marisol or if it was my mind merging the two girls.

When I woke, I'd go to my closet and take down the suitcase from the top shelf. I'd open it and randomly read through wishes, though I always made a point to read Marisol's— I'd added hers back in. I'd push my fingers through the scraps of paper, so that my hand was submerged, and I'd stir the wishes around. Even when I'd zipped up the suitcase and placed it back on the shelf, I'd hold those wishes in my heart, saving them for the moment I knew would come, when Isabel would emerge from the water and take them back.

A year passed. When I returned to Puerto Rico the next summer, the convent had been torn down, and I was forced to go with my dad to the hotel he'd been building in Rincón. He told me he'd never believed that I'd kidnapped those girls, that I was too much like my mother to do such a thing. He didn't explain what he meant by that. I was too sensitive? I was a coward? I didn't want to know, so I didn't ask.

We'd struck a deal: in exchange for taking a gap year, I'd work for him for room and board. I became a builder, spending most of my days with the foul-mouthed crew, hammering nails in the warm sun, laying pipe, pouring concrete. On my days off, I would stand at the water's edge, staring at that blue-green ocean and trying and failing to summon spirits.

Rico and Ruben came out for a week. Carlos wasn't with them. He'd saved up enough working at the convent to move to Chicago. He'd been gone since winter. My friends rarely heard from him, though they told me every month he would send a little money back to his mother and abuela.

Ruben was different, quieter. He said that Celia was doing all right. She didn't talk much about the doctor or her time at in the cabin, but every once in a while she'd mention wanting to go back to the western edge of the island to visit the other girls, the ones who she said came out of the water at night. She wanted to be there to greet them. She said they were lonely. I wanted to ask Ruben if she ever made him dizzy or sick to his stomach when he's around her for too long, but that isn't the type of thing you ask someone.

One night in Rincón, after Ruben had fallen asleep in my room in front of the television, Rico told me that all the plants in the courtyard of the house at the end of Calle Sol had died. One day they were alive, the next, wilted. I think he expected me to be sad, but I wasn't. The señoras once told me that the same thing had happened before, but that after a while the plants came back taller and thicker. I told Rico to wait and see, that in time those plants would be back. He nodded, said *sure, sure*, but I knew he didn't believe me.

I spent the night after Rico and Ruben left sitting alone on the beach. The air was unusually thick, and my ears were filled with murmurs from the sea and the trees.

I didn't hear the sound of the boy's feet kicking through sand as he approached, but when I looked over my shoulder, there he was. He had to have been about eight or nine years old, with ears that stuck out past his short-cropped dark hair.

In his outstretched hand was a small piece of paper, folded along a neat crease.

"Qué es esto?" I asked.

"Es para tí."

I pointed at my chest. "For me? De veras?"

He dropped the piece of paper at my feet and took off down the shoreline, toward the flickering lights of a string of small houses in the distance. I unfolded the note, but the light was too dim and the handwriting too bad for me to see what it said. I would have to wait until I got back to my room before I could read it and put it with all the others.

I went back to that story in my head, the one I'd started late last summer and had been building upon ever since. It started with a witch who could grant wishes. There were parts in the middle about girls who disappeared in the night, spirits who guarded a great island, and a scientist gone mad with grief. Two girls I would never get the chance to love would die; both their bodies would get swept out to sea with a storm.

But that won't be the end. One of the girls will come back. She'll walk out of the water just before dawn. I'll be waiting for her. She'll clutch the front of my shirt with her wet hands, pull me toward her, and kiss me with a mouth that tastes like saltwater. She will be warm.

THE END

ACKNOWLEDGMENTS

Many thanks to . . .

my champions: Krestyna Lypen, Elise Howard, and the team at Algonquin Young Readers; Michelle Andelman, Claire Anderson-Wheeler, and all at Regal Hoffman.

my teachers, including but certainly not limited to, Dennis Covington, Lad Tobin, and Paula Lemmon (*gratias tibi*).

my parents and family, all the Mabrys, Garcias, Schulzes, and Clarks.

my friends, particularly those who offered kind, brutal, and necessary feedback on early drafts of this manuscript.

my colleagues and students who spend their days in English classrooms.

my Jay.